Lilly Lord

Guy Lane

Chapters

Happiness in Hyperdrive

The theatre in the Sydney Opera House is packed, and the atmosphere is electric. Twenty-three hundred women, aged between 18 and 80, fill the auditorium to see motivational speaker Kara Lord.

Bathed in limelight, Kara Lord steps on stage, glistening like white fireworks as the spotlight strikes the sequins on her cocktail dress. A shock of curly, black hair wavers as she moves to the centre of the stage; a slim microphone poised in front of her mouth. She opens her arms to welcome the audience.

"My friends. My dear friends." Her words send the audience into a rapture of applause. Kara Lord settles the crowd with a well-honed movement of her hands.

"You're all living in a bubble," she tells them. She stands motionless, watching the women in the audience fall silent. The auditorium hushes as hundreds of people wait for her next words.

"You are all living in a big, beautiful bubble."

In a stall overlooking both the stage and the audience, Kara's elder sister, Lilly Lord, aged fifty-five, sits with her girlfriend Vinnie. Tonight, as always, Lillie and Vinnie, are thick as thieves. Vinnie has just returned from a six-week overseas holiday, and the two women have much to catch up on.

They are dressed in the manner that one would expect of ultra-wealthy women. Every detail, from the tips of their toenails to the top of the uppermost hair on their heads says out-loud, we are elite; do not come near us, unless you are like us.

Lilly and Vinnie don't just wear wealth; they're composed of it. Lilly's net worth is over one hundred million dollars because she is a co-founder and a major shareholder in *Chartreuse Capital* - a hedge fund devoted to fossil fuel companies - that she established with her husband over twenty years ago. In comparison, Vinnie is a pauper. If she were forced to sell everything, she'd be able to rustle-up no more than twenty million. Vinnie has taken this simple arithmetic to mean that Lilly is her superior, and that Lilly always gets to sit in the paying seat.

Lilly made her money through a keen business mind and the exponential growth of wealth that comes when you reach a critical threshold; if you are rich enough, you get richer without having to try. On the other hand, the source of Vinnie's wealth is good bone structure, a nice figure, and wise investments in husbands. Where Lilly picks fossil fuel stocks and analysts, Vinnie picks husbands and divorce lawyers.

Lilly retrieves a small pair of binoculars from her handbag. These are not regular binoculars, but antiques; theatre binoculars said to have been owned by Catherine the Great. She polishes the lenses in a well-rehearsed routine.

"Did she say bubbles?" asks Vinnie, coming alert.

"Yes," sighs Lilly. "Apparently, we all live in one."

"There'll be bubbles living in me, when I get home after this. Gosh, I'm craving a drink."

"We'll get a white in the foyer, after the show," Lilly suggests.

"That means we'll have to stand in the crowd."

"Oh, come on."

"And I'm driving, remember."

"Just the one, then."

Lilly extends the telescopic arm of the binoculars and studies her younger sister, intently. "She's put on weight."

Intrigued, Vinnie reaches for the glasses. "Incredible," she mutters. "How can she put on weight and still look like that?"

On the stage, Kara continues. "There are three types of happiness. I call them shits & giggles, meaningful duties, and true purpose. You can get shits & giggles anywhere, but they don't last. They just don't last."

"I can't believe what that woman's wearing on her head," Vinnie grumbles, fixing her gaze on an individual in the crowd.

"Let me see." Lilly takes the binoculars back. "Where?"

"Down there, look. Between the whales."

"Oh, dear. It's just wrong on every level."

"There is absolutely nothing fascinating about that fascinator," Vinnie grumbles. "Apart from how fugly it is."

Kara continues her pitch. "Another form of happiness comes from meaningful duties. That's your work and family."

Vinnie leans towards Lilly, "How are *you* going with your meaningful duties?"

"I sent Maxipus to Norfolk Island, the other day."

"Which one is Maxipus?"

"The red cat."

"I can't believe that you send your cat on holidays. You're such an innovator."

"He comes back so relaxed."

Kara continues her performance, "True purpose is the third way of getting happiness. You need something big and juicy to get your teeth into."

"Oh, this thing goes on forever." Vinnie fans herself with the event brochure.

"She's very good, though, isn't she?" Lilly asks.

"She's your sister, so I'll say yes."

Kara completes her opening sequence, "And if you can get all three types of happy, that's what puts your happiness into hyper-drive."

After the show, Lilly and Vinnie wait in the lobby, each holding a glass of white wine.

"Are you going backstage to say 'hi' to your sister?" Vinnie asks, as she mistrustfully watches the audience mingling in the foyer.

"Oh, I don't know. It's been a while since we've spoken. I'm not sure I want to have the first conversation like this. It was a good show, though. Don't you think?"

Vinnie hedges, shaking her head, "The content's a bit old."

"You think?"

"Did you see the review in the Herald?"

"What did it say?"

"Vapid, but entertaining."

"Vapid?" asks Lilly, surprized.

"As in empty."

"That's not true. She's encouraging us to find our true purpose, to hyper-drive happiness into our lives. That's a lovely sentiment."

"But can you trust the source?"

"What does that mean?"

"I mean, what is her true purpose?"

"To help other people find *their* true purpose."

"Not convinced, sorry." Vinnie shakes her head.

"Well, I'm watching a lot of people leaving that auditorium looking very happy, indeed," Lilly says, defensively.

"They looked pretty happy going in, as I recall."

"Maybe." Lilly looks at her empty glass. "Anothery?"

"I can't. I'm driving the wrong Mercedes."

"The one with the booze detector?"

"The damned thing. I should have it replaced."

"What with?" Lilly asks.

"A mini-bar."

They both laugh, and then look forlornly at their empty glasses.

"What happened to the other Mercedes?" Lilly asks.

"It hasn't been washed for a week."

"You're kidding."

Vinnie starts to wind up, "The car guy calls and says that his wife was having a baby, or something, and that he wasn't going to wash the car."

"Well, he's fired," Lilly says. "It's so hard to get good help."

"Tell me about it. I was like… *What…?*"

"I can imagine."

"*Anyhoo...*" Vinnie says, shaking her head. "Come on, let's get home."

"What do we do with the empties?" Lilly looks around for a surface to place it on.

"I'll sort that out." Vinnie takes the empty glass and drops it into a rubbish bin, along with her own. "Handled."

They walk to the underground car park where the valet retrieves the late-model Mercedes. He parks the vehicle about three meters away. "There you are, Miss," he hands over the keys.

"It is a bit far away, isn't it?" Vinnie protests.

"I'm sorry Ma'am?"

"I'm not wearing the right shoes for hiking." The valet looks back to the vehicle to determine what he's done wrong. The car could probably be moved half a meter closer. So, he moves it as requested, while Vinnie stands there shaking her head, indignantly.

Free from the concrete car park of the Sydney Opera House, Lilly and Vinnie speed towards the northern Sydney suburb of Duffys Forest, and the conversation resumes.

Vinnie asks, "When was the last time you saw your husband, Tom?"

"About a month ago. He's got a new helicopter."

"Another one?"

"He upgrades whenever a new model comes out."

"What colour is it?"

"Black," Lilly says.

"*Tut.* If he was going to buy a helicopter, you'd think that he'd get a nice colour."

"He drives me crazy with that thing," Lilly becomes annoyed, changing the position of her handbag on her lap. "He flies in, in the middle of the night, and lands the damned thing on the lawn."

"Didn't you just have that lawn re-laid?"

"Yes. I never did like that shade of green."

"What colour is it now?"

"Lime. At least it was. I had it ripped up and rose bushes flown in from Japan – ones with big thorns. So now there's a rose garden in his landing spot." Lilly laughs. "That'll teach him."

"Lilly, you are such a go-getter."

"You have to be firm, Vinnie. You have to hold your ground."

Vinnie nods at length, and then asks, "Have you seen your other sister, Rae?"

Lilly looks down at her handbag, resting on her lap. At first it is barely visible in the low light. Then the streetlights slip past, their light rising and falling, matching the ebb and flow of emotions that Lilly feels as she considers her other estranged sister. She enunciates the feeling with the noise, "*Hmmm.*"

"What's that?" Vinnie asks, glancing aside.

"My private investigator tells me that she is doing a presentation next week."

"Your P. I.?"

"Yes. I thought that if the auditorium was big enough, I might go along. You want to come?"

"Is it catered?" Vinnie asks.

"Probably not. It's some environmental thing. They've never got any money."

"Is she still into that?"

"Oh, yes. Big time," Lilly is now enthused to be talking about her younger sister. "They call her a thought-leader."

"Who'd have thought?" Vinnie scoffs. "So, what does she think about?"

"Something called transition."

"Sounds like a make-up. So, who's your P.I.?"

"He has an office in Dee Why," Lilly says. "He's quite good, actually. Chad Thompson."

Vinnie becomes animated. "He's my P.I."

"No. Really?"

"I've been using him for years."

"No way," Lilly says. "I never knew."

"You see, this is why you and I hang out together. Synchronicity."

"I guess," Lilly concedes.

In the hills in the northern suburbs of Sydney, Vinnie turns the car off the highway, and drives through the estates of Duffys Forest.

Up ahead, there is an orange flashing light. A vehicle is parked on the side of the road and the driver is changing a flat tyre. Vinnie pulls up, waiting for oncoming traffic to pass.

In the distance, beyond the parked car, a young man walks in their direction.

"Funny night to be taking a walk," Vinnie says, leaning forward to better see him.

He is in his late twenties, wearing a hoodie, and he walks face-down, looking at the ground in front of him. His face is hidden in shadow, but becomes visible for just a second, as he passes the car.

"Don't even think about it," Vinnie says.

"What?"

"Young and handsome, black, curly hair. A sort of lost, ravenous look."

"Oh, come on. As if I am on the prowl. I'm married, Vinnie."

"Of course, you are." Vinnie chuckles. It's an old joke that never seems to run dry.

"You know who that is, don't you?" Lilly asks.

"He's too well dressed to be a feral. Do you recognise him?"

"I'm trying to think of his name. He used to live around here. He had a strange name. Like a psychologist, or something."

"Clarkeson?" suggests Vinnie.

"I don't mean your psychologist."

"Jung?"

"No."

"Freud?"

"Froyd," Lilly says. "His name is Froyd Denison."

"Froyd Denison," Vinnie murmurs, thinking it through. "I remember. There was a huge scandal, years ago. An unmarried mother."

"It's just so wrong," Lilly sighs.

"And the speculation about who the father was."

Lilly watches Froyd through wing mirror as he fades into the night. "It's a bit strange, isn't it?"

"What?"

"That he'd be wandering around like that."

"*Anyhoo…*" Vinnie says, moving on. "When did you last speak to her?"

"Who?"

"Your green sister, Rae."

"Oh, yes, Rae. She dissed me on my birthday."

"That's right. You were going to fly her to the party."

"The private jet used too much fuel for her liking, apparently."

"What? That's crazy."

"Fee trip to Hayman Island. She just blew it off."

"What is wrong with that girl?"

Vinnie pulls the Mercedes up to driveway of Lilly's mansion as the white security gate slides open. She drives inside, parking in front of the house. Something takes her attention, and she leans forward, peering through the window, "You've had it painted, again."

"Couldn't take to the shade. It just wasn't beige enough."

"Are you going to be okay, alone in that empty house?"

"It's hardly empty. It has a wine cellar and a box set of Master Chef."

"You should be alright then. Lunch tomorrow? Church Point? My shout."

"Okay. I'll drive," Lilly offers.

"Good. I'll drink. Which car?"

"If you are going to drink seriously," says Lilly. "Take a Bentley."

The Jellybean

Mid-morning, Lilly is seated in her chair by the bay windows in the lounge room, wearing a dressing gown. She looks across the gardens, taking particular satisfaction in the helicopter-denying rose bushes. They are formidable, with thick stems, and harsh, sharp thorns.

She calls the spot where she sits her *cocoon*. It has everything that she needs. The primary feature is an ornate armchair, formerly owned by a Viennese aristocrat. On the right side of the chair is an Apple Mac computer connected to the internet that allows her to conduct business, shop online, and go on long web-surfing sessions that sometimes take her to places that she subsequently wishes she'd never been.

On the other side of the chair is a drinks service trolley with an ice bucket. It contains a dazzling array of plonk from every corner of the world. Despite the choice, Lilly is quite reserved in her drinking, preferring a few varieties of white wine from a small collection of Australian wineries and a particular red from a vineyard in Brazil.

In front of the seat is a large, flat screen TV and home entertainment system. It is all top of the range, connected together by experts.

Lilly's cocoon overlooks the landscaped grounds at the back of her house. These extend several hundred meters to a wall beyond which is the thickly forested national park.

If one were ever to look for Lilly Lord, she would most likely be found in this location, sitting in her cocoon, occupied by her entertainments. She might be watching TV, browsing the internet, listening to the radio or to music, or watching a movie.

Other times, you might find her staring into space, a glass of $100-a-bottle white wine in hand, numbly wondering what had happened to her life.

Another advantage of Lilly's cocoon is that it affords a vantage point from which to spy on her hired help. The theatre binoculars are always positioned close by, allowing her to keep a watchful eye on the workers. One of her particular interests is whether the young tradesmen wear matching socks. Unmatched socks are an instant dismissal offence, and no small number of workers has been sent home for breaking this unwritten rule.

This morning, Lilly has no workers to spy on, and instead, she is googling for additional means to prevent the incursion of helicopters. She inadvertently finds herself on a Russian weapon manufacturers website. While she has no plans to buy military equipment, she is nonetheless fascinated by the dazzling array of options. The prices all seem very reasonable, too.

She learns that one effective means of helicopter

denial involves blasting it from the sky with a shoulder launched missile. Lilly watches with morbid fascination as a young Russian soldier fires on a chopper from a turret in the roof of a black military truck.

"Oh, dear," she says, shocked, putting her fingers to her mouth. She closes the webpage, and then deletes the recent history from the browser.

At half past midday, she changes into her luncheon clothes, and goes to the garage. As the overhead lights flicker on, five cars come into view. The red Ferrari Berlinetta and the E-Type jaguar belong to her husband, so they're off limits. That leaves the black Bentley Continental, the black Mercedes SLK, and the orange Mazda MX5.

Lilly affectionately refers to the Mazda as the Jellybean because its rounded shape gives it a vague resemblance to the lolly. Jellybeans also come in a variety of colours, and this car has variously been coloured red, yellow, blue and now orange over its short life.

Something about having watched the Russian soldiers shoot down the helicopter from a black truck unnerves Lilly about the two black cars, and so she takes the Jellybean keys from the rack. She refers to the log that has been filled out by the vehicle maintenance guy to see that it has been fuelled and recently detailed. It all checks out, so the Jellybean, it is.

Before she goes to the car, she checks herself in the full-length mirror, and realises that she is dressed for the Bentley. This won't do. So, she returns to her room, strips off her dress and drops it into the bin marked with the words 'dry clean'. She dons a dress and jewellery that is fitting for the orange sports car.

Back in the garage, she steps into the Jellybean. With the key in the ignition, the car syncs with her smartphone. She opens the app for the remote control, and watches in the rear vision mirror as the garage door lifts up. Then a fan starts up, blowing a jet of air across the vehicle to push the exhaust out of the garage; she can't stand the smell of vehicle exhaust.

Then she fires the engine and waits thirty seconds during which time she puts on her driving gloves and glasses. When the engine is warm, she backs out of the garage and activates the app to close up. She watches the garage doors close as she drives to the main gate. This opens on her command, and then closes behind her. Lilly turns the Jellybean onto the road, accelerates, and she's away.

When she is a hundred meters from the property, the app sends push notifications to key staff, alerting them that Lilly has left the property. They are now free to come out of the corners and do their work. With the technology enabling her introversion, Lilly is able to live her pampered life having to interact with almost no-one but her closest friend. The family is at arms-length; the staff are at arms-length. She is free.

She tells the smartphone, "Call Vinnie," and like all the people who tend to her, the phone promptly complies.

Vinnie answers, and Lilly tells her, "I'm in the Jellybean. I'll be about fifteen minutes."

"The Jellybean? I thought you said the Bentley. Is it still orange?"

"For now."

"Damn, I am going to have to change. Oh, and Lilly?"

"What?"

"Have I got news for you?"

Church Point Lunch

The restaurant overlooks the Pittwater. The *Maitre d'* shows Lilly and Vinnie to their regular spot.

The first order is the wine, and once that is poured, Vinnie retrieves a folder from her bag, lays it on the table, and taps it with a fingernail repeatedly until she has Lilly's attention. "Guess who has been doing some research?"

"Research on what?"

"You remember our rendezvous last night? Young Master Denison."

"You have been researching him?"

Vinnie nods knowingly. "Oh, boy. What a scandal. And a what a mystery."

"Really?" now Lilly is intrigued.

"This is not yet the full picture."

"What have you found?"

" Are you sitting down?"

" Apparently."

"We're going back in time now, about twenty-five years. A certain Ms. Denison from Dee Why has a girlfriend who lives in Bayview. Ms. Denison takes a liking to the area. So, she puts on her lippy and high-heels and gets herself knocked-up by a local man."

"Who?"

"To this day, he remains unnamed. What does she do next? She blackmails him into funding her lifestyle, which includes buying a property in Terrey Hills. Young Froyd Denison, raised in the home of this heavy drinking charlatan, somehow manages to get accepted into a finance degree at Monash, only to go off-grid before the exams in his final year."

"Off grid, what does that mean?" asks Lilly, perplexed.

"Vanishes from the record," Vinnie says in a conspiratorial whisper.

"Where are you getting this information from?"

"Various sources. Cheryl, mainly. And I did some googling. Made some calls. You want to hear the rest of it?"

"There's more?."

"So, next thing, it turns out that Ms. Denison has one vat of wine too many and keels over from liver disease about three months ago."

"That's why he came back," Lilly says. She sits back in her seat, taking it all in.

A young waiter, who looks like he's about twelve, interrupts them. He's wearing black pants, white shirt, and a blue and white vertically striped apron. He has his pad and pen poised to take an order. "Could I offer an entrée," he asks.

"Yes," Vinnie picks up the menu and points to one of the items. "Here, the bruschetta with Tasmanian salmon, capers, cracked pepper, drizzled with aioli."

"Certainly, Ma'am. Two serves of this?"

"Actually, with the salmon, could you change that to sashimi yellow-fin. And no capers, I hate capers."

"Certainly, Ma'am."

"And swap the cracked pepper with Red Sea Salt."

"Okay, Ma'am." The waiter scribbles, trying to keep up.

"Oh, and no bruschetta. Just put it on sour dough. And that tuna, actually, do you have Big-eye?"

"I think so, Ma'am. Just the one of these?"

"What do you reckon?" Vinnie asks Lilly.

"Oh, I'll try it. I'll try it."

"Two of those." Vinnie watches the waiter depart and she makes a grim smile. "That'll mess them up," she chuckles, cruelly.

With the distraction over, Lilly goes straight back the scandalous mystery. "So, he came back to say bye to mum and wrap up the estate?"

"I guess. So now there is an orphaned waif

wandering around the forest who is the heir to millions in Terrey Hills real estate."

"How much, do you reckon?"

"I talked to Casey, the estate agent. She says that Denison bought the property for $3.5 million. That was over twenty years ago."

"It would be worth ten plus now," Lilly says. "I wonder if she had any cash."

"*Nah*. She drank it all."

Lilly sits back in her seat. She nods her head a few times as she mulls over the mystery of Froyd Denison. "Good work. Well, I'm glad that's settled."

"Settled. What, are you kidding me?"

"No?"

"Who is the father, Lilly? Where did he go during this off-grid period? What did he do? Why was he wandering around Duffys Forest at 11pm the other night? Where's he sleeping? Who's he sleeping with? And why? These things are all unresolved." Vinnie taps the manila folder. "This is just the beginning." She clasps the glass of Chardonnay and lubricates her throat, ready to begin again. "So, you want to hear my plan?"

"You have that look again," Lilly says, breaking a smile.

"What look?"

"It's mischievous. Devious. Up to no good."

"It's 'my' true purpose. You want to hear the plan?"

"Of course, I want to hear the plan."

"So, we get your private investigator, and my private investigator onto the job."

"But we both use the same private investigator."

"Exactly, so we spilt the bill fifty-fifty."

Lilly waves her hand. "Oh, don't be silly."

"How's that silly? Don't you want you know?"

"It's…"

"What?"

"It's indulgent," Lilly says.

"Indulgent? Really, Lilly?" Vinnie sounds offended.

"What?"

"You send your pets on holiday."

"So?"

"And you change the colour of your assets like some women change lipstick."

Lilly furrows her brow, not liking this turn of the conversation. She takes a sip of her wine. "Well, I guess it would be good to know who is wandering around the neighbourhood in the middle of the night."

"Exactly"

"How much would it cost, do you think?"

"We'll cap it at ten thousand dollars. Five each."

Lilly hesitates for a while. "Oh, hell! Why not? What's ten thousand dollars, anyway?" Lilly says, knowing that she'll end up paying the whole bill. "Let's do this thing."

"Excellent!" Vinnie raises her glass to toast.

"What are we toasting, then?"

"Pulling the covers off Froyd Denison's affairs."

Vehicle Inspection

After lunch, instead of taking the normal way home, Lilly drives a longer route, one that takes her along some forested roads. Vinnie's insistence on the mystery of Froyd Denison has worked into her mind and she's curious to learn more. While she's not actively looking for Froyd Denison, she is leaving herself open to a chance encounter.

She drives around for half an hour or so, and eventually comes to the road that runs past her home. As she approaches the gate she notices that the hedge in front of the wall has been growing again. It is no longer flat and rectangular like in the brochure.

"What is it with that damned hedge?" she says aloud. "Note to self. Get the gardener onto the hedges. Again."

Then, she has a second wind, and speeds up, driving past her gate, continuing with her passive search.

Two kilometres further along she slows, her heart racing. Something tells her that she is closing in on her quarry. The phone rings and she accepts the call.

Vinnie's voice chimes over the speakers, "Done it."

"Done what?"

"I've booked Chad Thompson. He says he'll get straight onto it."

"Well, that's great." Lilly slows the vehicle, the indicator ticking as she approaches a dirt road that leads off to the left. The wheels of the car hit the gravel on the edge of the tarmac.

"You are still driving?" Lilly asks.

"Sort of."

"Don't tell me you've caught the bug."

"What are you talking about?"

"Where are you?"

"I'm just approaching Robert's Road. Oh my God." Lilly hits the brakes, and the tyres lock up, skidding on the gravel."

"Are you okay?" asks Vinnie.

"*Shhh!*" Lilly hisses.

"What's the matter?"

"It's him."

Twenty meters away, walking towards her, is Froyd Denison. He approaches steadily, his eyes fixed on the car.

Lilly freezes, not knowing what to do. She watches as Froyd comes closer, his eyes moving onto hers. She feels self-conscious, and blushes, then makes a forced grin as if everything is okay.

Froyd wears a Tom Ford overcoat, chino pants and R&B boots, his clothing is stylish, but worse for wear. His curly black hair partly covers his face, adding to the mystique. He has shadows under his eyes, a gaunt look, and an overall appearance of a moneyed Che Guevara, fallen on hard times. He halts a few meters from the car and leans forward to examine it in detail.

"What's happening?" whispers Vinnie, over the phone.

"*Shhh,*" Lilly hisses, watching Froyd intently.

He delves into his pocket and retrieves a sheet of paper and a pen. He folds the paper in his palm and then inscribes on to it. He walks around the car, and Lilly follows his progress through the mirrors. Having conducted a 360-degree assessment of the vehicle, he comes alongside the driver's door and gently raps a knuckle on the glass.

"Oh, Dear," she says.

"What's happening?"

"*Shhh*!" Lilly winds the electric window part way down. "Hello. Yes?" she asks anxiously.

"Hello, Ma'am," Froyd says, lightly. "I am conducting a Planetary Boundaries assessment of your vehicle. Do you mind if I ask a few questions?"

"*Ummm*. Sorry. What is it, exactly?"

"A Planetary Boundaries assessment of your

vehicle. It's just a few questions. If you don't mind."

"Well, that's fine, I guess."

"Is this your car?"

"It is."

"Did you choose it yourself?"

"Yes."

"And how is it powered. Electric charged with solar energy, maybe?"

"No. It's petrol."

"Petrol? *Uh-huh*?"

"Unleaded petrol, that is," Lilly says, hoping that somehow makes it better.

"Airbags?"

"Of course."

"*Uh-huh.*" Froyd makes a final few inscriptions on his paper. Then he unfolds the document and hands it to Lilly.

"Negative six. You could do better than that, Mrs Lord," Froyd says. Then, with that cryptic comment hanging in the air, he continues on his way.

Lilly watches as he moves on, walking along the road in the direction of her house, a few kilometres away. She winds up the window and lets out a long sigh.

"Has he gone?" Vinnie hisses over the phone.

"What happened?"

"I'm not really sure."

"What does negative six mean?"

"He wrote something on a piece of paper and served me with it." Lilly looks at the document in her hand, trying to make sense of its meaning.

"Lilly. You are to bring that piece of paper to me immediately."

Lilly considers the idea of returning home, which would involve driving past Froyd Denison again. "I'll be there shortly."

Vita Website

Over a glass of wine at Vinnie's kitchen table, Lilly repeats the story of her encounter with Froyd a third time. This time, Vinnie is satisfied that she has gotten the last piece of information, and she turns her attention to the document that Lilly had been served with.

It is a single sheet, printed both sides with the word DRAFT in watermark running diagonally. It is titled: P. B. Checklist. On the front page is a diagram, a circle sliced into nine pieces. Each slice is coloured differently with reds and greens and yellow. Around the perimeter of the circle, are words, naming each of the slices. Adjacent to some of these words, Froyd has written a number, either a (-1) or a (-3). From the top of the diagram moving clockwise, it says:

- Climate Change (-3)
- Novel Entities (-1)
- Stratospheric Ozone Depletion (-1)
- Atmospheric Aerosol Loading
- Ocean Acidification (-1)
- Biogeochemical Flows: Phosphorous / Nitrogen
- Freshwater Use
- Land System Change
- Biosphere Integrity: Functional / Genetic Diversity

On the reverse side of the sheet is a table in which

Froyd has tallied all the numbers, summing the total to negative six. Beneath this, a block of text in small letters offers a description of each of the nine titles.

"Well, that's absolutely meaningless," Vinnie says, dismissively.

"What about this?" Lilly taps her fingernail against the logo at the top of the page.

The logo shows three circles that overlap in such a manner as to form a three-pointed star in the middle, like the blades of a wind turbine. Around the outside of these circles, is an incomplete ring, the lower section missing.

Under the logo is a single word: Vita and the web address: *vitasapien.org*.

"*Hmmm,*" Vinnie says at last, as if all this information actually means something to her. She raises the bottle of South Australian Chablis. "Anothery?"

"I shouldn't. I'm driving. Let's check out the website. Where's your tablet?"

Vinnie retrieves an ipad and enters the web address. The page loads, and she slides the tablet around so that they can both see the screen.

Lilly recites the words on the top of the page: *"Based on science & common sense, Vita is an integrated system of belief, knowledge & practice that is devoted to sustainability & happiness. Join the Vita People today."*

"You got a negative six for sustainability from Froyd God Almighty," Vinnie scoffs.

"I got off lightly, then."

"The big question that I have out of all of this..." Vinnie says, leaving her words hanging in the air.

Lilly folds the paper and slides it into her purse. "What's the big question?"

"Well..." Vinnie says, thinking it through. "Didn't Froyd say to you: *You could do better than that, Mrs Lord.*"

"That's right."

"So how does he know your name?"

Froyd Fell in Frack Fluid

Over the next few days, the mystery of Froyd Denison deepens. Vinnie's question, "How does Froyd know my name?" keeps ringing through her head. On one hand, it is spooky. On the other, she feels privileged to have attracted his attention. To try and get to the bottom of it all, Lilly retires to her cocoon, and undertakes a thorough review of the thinkvita.org website.

There is a lot of content, allowing for hours of browsing. There are explainer videos on Vita spiritual philosophy that discuss all manner of ideas new to Lilly. There is the oft repeated word 'Anthropocene', Blue Ocean Event, Planetary Boundaries, the Sixth & human extinction. It all sounds rather grim, and yet it is all conveyed with a smile and a straight face. It's quite unnerving, really.

Vinnie calls, excitedly, saying that the private investigator has reported back with news. Half an hour later she arrives, enlivening the house.

When Lilly returns from the kitchen with the wine and glasses, Vinnie is looking through the bay windows at the helicopter-denying rose garden. The plants are scantily clad with leaves and flowers. Most noticeable are the sinewy stems bearing pointy thorns. Row upon row of deadly bushes bristle like razor wire on a battlefield.

Vinnie turns, an ashen look on her face. "You were serious about those rose bushes, weren't you?"

"Area denial, they call it," Lilly says, lightly, pulling the cork from the bottle with a $900 corkscrew that she bought online from a Los Angeles art gallery. "It's a military design that I picked up online."

Vinnie shakes her head and takes a seat, "*Anyhoo...*" She holds her glass.

Lilly pours the wine. "So, what's news?"

"The plot has thickened. Are you ready for this?"

"Hold on. Let me get settled in." Lilly makes herself comfy in her chair. With her elbow, she accidentally nudges the mouse connected to her computer. The monitor alights, showing the last thing that she was watching. This is a documentary on Near Term Extinction, the grimmest concept of all from the Vita website.

Lilly likes to keep her grim viewing to herself and seeing the image on the screen makes her feel self-conscious. She promptly turns off the monitor. "So, what have we found out?"

"Well, you remember how Froyd dropped out of a prestigious university just before his finals?"

"Yes, I remember."

"It turns out that he got radicalised by a woman."

"Really? Who?"

"Don't know yet. But they had some torrid affair, after which he goes off and becomes some sort of eco-guru. Last heard of doing something called… Hold on, I wrote it down." Vinnie delves into her purse to retrieve a post-it note that is covered in scrawl. "Monkey wrenching. Whatever that is."

"Sabotage for the purpose of environmental protection," Lilly says, knowingly.

Vinnie eyes the rose bushes suspiciously, "Right. And how would you know that?"

"Oh, you know?" Lilly brushes a bit of fluff off her trouser leg, looking away. She knows because she read it on the Vita website, and she watched the youtube videos, too.

"*Anyhoo*… Froyd and his eco-terrorist mates were in central Queensland on a monkey-wrenching mission and something nasty happened to him."

"What happened?" Lilly asks, suddenly concerned.

"Hang on. I wrote it down." Vinnie refers to the post-it again. She twists it this way and that, trying to interpret the scrawl. "Chad called late, you see. I'd had a few. Here it is. He fell into a vat of… What's that say?"

"Let me have a look," says Lilly, anxious for an answer.

"I've got it. I've got it. Fracking fluid."

"What?"

"Froyd fell into fracking fluid. *Huh!* Try saying that three times with a bottle white in you."

"What is that?"

"I don't know. But apparently, it's nasty stuff. Chad found a medical report from the Queensland Police."

"The police?"

"Yes. Froyd was arrested. He was treated inside. He was really sick, apparently. Nearly died."

"Oh, my gosh." Lilly puts her fingertips to her mouth. "He did look rather ill. Gaunt, with shadows under his eyes."

"Well, there you have it. Some *femme fatale* suckered him into a life of environmental crime, and it didn't pay off."

"Well, that's just fascinating." Lilly sits back in her chair, fulfilled by the information. "Anything else?"

"That's all for now. Apart from an invoice."

"I'll take care of that." Lilly reaches over and takes the bill from Vinnie.

Later, when Vinnie has left, Lilly sits, staring out at the rose bushes, contemplating the mystery of Froyd Denison. Finally, she comes out of her trance and goes back to Vita website. She finds a video on abrupt climate change that is grim enough to satisfy her morbid curiosity.

The video shows computer-generated images of cyclones rapidly intensifying, and news footage of the storms delivering punishing, freak weather events on an unsuspecting and vulnerable population. Lilly is fascinated by the macabre power of the super-storms, so she watches intently. She feels very lucky to have come across a new and fascinating diversion from the golden dullness of her life.

Finally, at 7 pm, it is time for ABC News, and she drifts off to sleep in front of the TV. She wakes to see the weather woman waving her arms in front of a weather map that bears a striking resemblance to the one in the abrupt climate change video.

Lilly retrieves the remote control and increases the volume. A severe rain event is forecasted, starting soon. The computer-generated image looks like an angry welt that covers half of New South Wales, a swirling mass of red and purple

Through the bay windows, Lilly sees a flicker of lightning in the distance. She thinks about Froyd Denison, and she wonders where he is living, and whether he will be out of the rain when it comes.

Drambuie in the Rain

The next morning, Lilly wakes to the sound of the downpour. She lies in bed listening to the rain. She wonders how Froyd is coping, and what he was doing in Roberts Road, when she last saw him.

It is rare to hear rain in her room, as the house is so heavily constructed. Plus, the 24-hour per day air-conditioning unit does make a noise, despite what the brochure said. The words 'extreme weather' come to mind, and she ponders what that means for the people who don't live in million-dollar mansions.

After breakfast, she braves the inclement weather and takes the Bentley for a spin. On the road, the rain hammers down, pushed around by the wind that comes in sharp, confused gusts. A normal car would be nearly impossible to drive in these conditions, but the Bentley has top of the range everything, including industrial strength windscreen wipers.

Lilly drives in the rain for over an hour, investigating how the storm is affecting her neighbourhood. Then she drives down to Bayview and observes how the storm plays out over the Pittwater. She drives to coast, seeing the sea surface flattened by the rain, and the drab sky over the Pacific Ocean.

The storm intensifies, and she turns back for the

hills. Here, she finds that trees are down, torrents of water gush across the road, and powerlines swing ominously to-and-fro.

There are few vehicles on the road, and those that are, drive slowly, their headlights on. The noise of the rain is intense, hammering down on the Bentley's metal roof.

Finally, Lilly starts to think that her life would be improved if she were sitting in her cocoon drinking wine, so she turns the Bentley towards home.

As she drives along, out of the hazy distance, she sees a figure. She slows, conscious that her heart is racing. As she approaches, she makes the figure out to be a man in a black overcoat. She pulls alongside, peering through the side window.

Froyd is hunched up, the lapel of his jacket clenched in his fist and pushed against his chest. He is squinting to keep the rain out of his eyes, as he casts a glance in Lilly's direction.

She winds down the electric window a little way, calling out, "Is it Froyd Denison?" The noise of the rain is so intense that she has to shout to be heard.

Froyd halts. He leans forward and peers through the window. "Hello, Mrs Lord. You have another car."

"Froyd Denison?"

"It's nice to see you."

"Where are you going?"

"I'm going home."

"Can I give you a ride?"

"I'll ruin your upholstery. I'm drenched."

"I can get it replaced. Get in. You'll freeze to death."

Froyd stands up, and for a few seconds his face is lost from Lilly's view. Then he opens the car door and steps inside. With the door open, the cabin is filled with a swirl of wet, cold air. It is the first that Lilly has felt of the storm, having gotten into the Bentley inside the air-conditioned garage. When the door is closed, the swirl of air settles.

"Thanks for this," Froyd says.

"Where do you live?"

"Roberts Road. Where I saw you the other day."

"You were going to walk all the way there?"

"Yeah," Froyd chuckles. "But this is a much better idea, even though it is petrol-powered."

Lilly pulls out from the side of the road, accelerating the car, "I hear that this rain is going to break some records."

"Funny," Froyd says. "That's C3 on the Death Spiral, by the way." He digs around inside his jacket and retrieves a folded piece of paper, another Vita document.

Lilly glances at the paper. It has a circle with a

spiral inside, and words in boxes on a grid.

"There you go, see," Froyd taps the document with a pen. "Record breaking rain events. I'll tick that one off, for you." He strikes the paper with his pen, then folds it, and lodges the damp document in the dashboard. "You can fill the rest in later."

"Really."

"Yeah. Just watch the news."

"What happens when they are all ticked off?" Lilly asks.

"Human extinction. Unless Lilly Lord has an Ecophany, first." Froyd chuckles, looking directly at her.

"Do you always talk in riddles?"

"Only when it's not happening, Lilly."

"Right."

Lilly suddenly wonders whether it was such a good idea to pick Froyd up. Vinnie's intelligence report had made no reference to the state of his mental health.

"I had a look at the Vita Sapien website."

"Really?" Froyd is surprised.

"It's very interesting. So why are you living in the forest?"

"I wanted to get out of the bubble. Into the real world."

"The real world in a shack in the forest," Lilly

scoffs.

"We don't live in the world that 'is', Mrs Lord. We live in the world that we want it to be."

"Is that right?"

"Imagine that you have bought a lotto ticket, and you stand in the newsagency, clutching the piece of paper, saying to yourself 'this is a winning ticket, this is the winning ticket' over and over again. Can you imagine that?"

"Yes, I can."

"Does it make you any more likely to win, Lilly?"

"No, it doesn't."

"I can call you Lilly, can't I, Lilly?"

"How do you know my name?"

"Well, you're famous, Lilly."

"I am?" A little waft of vanity washes over her, and it feels nice, like champagne bubbles sparkling under her nose.

"I saw you on the cover of a magazine. The Queen of Coal, they called you."

"*Huh*. That was years ago."

"Anyway, what I was saying is that by living in the fantasy, we don't see the real odds. We don't see the wolves creeping up on us. So, the carbon builds in the atmosphere, acid grows in the sea, and it all ends in tears. Hot, salty, acidic tears."

"That's very philosophical," Lilly says, chuckling.

"You think that's amusing?"

"I didn't mean it that way. I like the poetry."

"Yeah. Well, I'm a poet, alright."

Lilly glances at Froyd, but he has turned his face towards the window and blocks her out. "I've lost him," Lilly thinks. "Boy, this guy is fractious."

Lilly turns the Bentley into Roberts Road. She has to concentrate on the dirt track, careful not to hit a pothole.

"Just up ahead here," Froyd says. "Turn into that gate."

Lilly enters the driveway and pulls up adjacent to a small red brick house. The garden is overgrown, and the house dilapidated. There is a solar panel leaning up against the wall, the cable snaking through the window. The heavy rain and the forest make the scene cold and dark.

"You live here?"

"Yeah. Cool huh? Would you come inside?"

"I'm not sure that's a good idea."

"I'd like it if you did, Lilly. I won't bite. Promise." Without waiting for her answer, Froyd steps out of the car and hurries to the porch, out of the rain. Lilly hesitates, not knowing what to do. Froyd beckons for her to come, and she smiles, suddenly feeling very young.

Something about Froyd reminds her of a happy

time in her life, when she was courting her husband, Tom. They were in France, in the Champagne region, of course. There was a storm, and they both got drenched running from the hire car to the villa.

"Oh, what the hell?" Lilly swings open the door and makes a dash for the front door. Froyd ushers her into the gloomy hallway.

"Hold up. I'll put the light on." He disappears into the dark lounge room. Then he directs her into the room where there is a single LED light hanging from a wire connected to the lampshade. It illuminates the centre of the room with a blue-white tinge.

"Sit." He points to a threadbare armchair. Then he fossicks around in a bag to retrieve a torch. "Back in a minute."

Lilly perches on the edge of the seat, peering anxiously around the room; she wonders how Froyd could maintain a positive mental attitude living in the frigid, musty cave. The room has more darkness than light, suggesting that there are unseen things in the periphery.

Visible is a second armchair with a makeshift workstation consisting of a laptop computer and printer. The floor is littered with printed documents, stapled top right and covered in coloured, hand-written notes.

Froyd returns to the lounge room. He's holding a glass and a small bottle.

"What are all the documents?" Lilly asks.

"Science papers."

"You're a scientist?"

"I guess."

"What are you doing with them?"

"Reading them. Absorbing their wisdom. Here we go." He passes over a champagne flute.

Lilly peers at the glass, checking it for cleanliness. There is insufficient light to properly determine whether it meets her standards.

Froyd unscrews the lid from a small 30 ml bottle of Drambuie, the scotch liqueur, and pours half of the bottle into Lilly's glass. As he concentrates on the pour he attempts a Scottish accent, "A wee dram to warm ye on a cold, wet day."

"Well, thank you." Lilly sniffs the glass. The liqueur is volatile, fruity and sweet, masking any odour that the glass may hold.

Froyd takes a swig from the bottle. "Oh, hell that's nice." He inhales deeply, and then exhales at length, sinking back into his seat, as though all his energy had departed him.

Lilly looks up at the white light and follows with her eyes the electrical cable the spans the room, wraps around the curtain rail, then descends to a car battery next to the window. "You don't have mains electricity?"

"*Nah,*" Froyd sighs.

"So, no hot water?"

"Lots of rainwater, but." Froyd chuckles at his own joke.

"You'll freeze to death."

"Not if I die of something else first."

"So, what is it you do here?"

"I'm working on a program, Lilly. I'm not sure that you want to know the truth of that, just yet."

"More riddles."

"It's a riddle, alright." Froyd's breathing sounds laboured. He snuggles himself into the seat, probably more to get warm than comfortable.

Lilly turns her attention to the documents on the floor. She lifts some of the papers, and flips through them, scanning the titles. Dark Green Religion. The Anthropocene. Civilization Collapse. Abrupt Climate Change. Devoted Actor Theory. Transition.

Transition! There's that word again. A word associated with her sister, Rae. She flips through the document, hoping that it will explain the word simply and quickly. She sees that it has something to do with climate change and the economy. Changing the economy to accommodate climate change concerns. She is about to ask Froyd to explain, but he has drifted off to sleep in his chair, the Drambuie bottle held against his chest.

"How extraordinary," Lilly thinks. She collects some more documents and scans the titles. Thermodynamics of Sustainability. Collapse of Marine Fisheries. The Sixth Extinction. Overcoming Climate Denial. Sustainability and the Superclass.

Lilly lowers the documents, exhausted just by reading the titles. She notices the torch on the arm of Froyd's chair.

Froyd lets out a gurgling snore, almost as if he were willing her to take the torch. Lilly steps into the hallway and scans the beam around the kitchen, the bathroom and Froyd's sleeping quarters. The room is empty except for a mattress on the floor with a doona and pillow. A piece of rope serves as a wardrobe for his clothes.

A shiver runs up Lilly's spine as she considers how it must be to live in this cold, dungeon-like house. She returns to the lounge room, sits in her chair and picks up her Drambuie. The liqueur is rich and spicy, perhaps the only thing that approaches warmth in the whole building.

"If had to live in this house, I'd fill the bathtub with warm Drambuie and soak in it," she thinks.

Froyd stirs in his sleep. It sounds as though fluid is building in his lungs as every inhalation is accompanied by a rasping noise. Lilly watches with grim fascination, wondering what comes next.

What comes next is a coughing fit. It is awful. Froyd wakes, choking, gasping for air. He struggles to retrieve a handkerchief from his pants pocket as he gags. He hacks into it the tissue and then glances at the material he has coughed up. He wipes blood off his chin and sits back, catching his breath, exhausted. Then he digs around in his pocket and retrieves a small vial. He taps a pale-yellow powder onto the back of his hand, presses a nostril closed with a finger, and then snorts the powder into the other nostril. He shakes his head like a wet dog, and the action helps him come back to life. He looks around and sees Lilly staring at him, aghast.

"Paprika," he says, chuckling.

Lilly leans forward, a grim look on her face. "Is that really paprika?"

"No, Lilly." Froyd laughs aloud.

"What is it, then?"

"Homebrew self-medication. And surprisingly effective."

"What's in it?"

"Can't tell you, sorry."

Lilly sits back, shaking her head. She is flustered, and astounded that anyone could live this way, and be so nonchalant about it. The boy is seriously ill and could easily die in these conditions. That will not happen on her watch.

A rarely seen side of Lilly Lord rises to the fore and she leans forward, pointing one of her manicured fingers directly at Froyd's face. In a forceful and thoroughly convincing tone, she growls, "Now listen to me Froyd Denison. You are not staying in this house tonight."

"No?"

"You are coming to my home where you will soak in a hot tub while I wash and dry your clothes. Tomorrow, I will return you to this cold, dark cave. But you are not dying here tonight. Do you understand?"

Froyd nods gravely. He coughs again and then shows an almost guilty look for having done so.

"So, get your stuff. We are leaving right now."

Minibar in the Bathroom

In the Bentley, with Froyd sitting beside her, Lilly drives slowly along the dirt track feeling like something seismic is taking place in her life. Caring for the sick young man makes her feel more purposeful than she has in a long time.

She glances across at Froyd and asks, with gravitas, "Do you have a diagnosed illness?"

"It's called mortality. It's coming for me."

"Is that because of the frack fluid?"

"You heard about that? That stuff is bad news, Lilly. We shouldn't be putting it in our aquifers. I still get this metallic taste in my mouth. It's awful."

"Is it cancer?"

"Yeah. Lots of it."

"How long do you have?"

"I was given six months. Assuming that I don't make my own plan."

"You have a plan to beat the cancer?"

"No, Lilly. That's not going to happen. I'll die 'with' cancer, not 'of' cancer."

"I don't understand."

"You will."

"And what's with all the science papers?"

"I'm completing a big protect before I go."

"Can you tell me about it?"

"It's you, Lilly."

"I'm sorry?"

"It's you, Lilly. You're my project."

Lilly feels a chill run through her body. It rushes up her spine and departs the top of her head, making her scalp tingle. She sees the skin turn to goose on her forearms, the hairs standing alert like antennae picking up a faint signal. Froyd's statement renders her mute.

One part of her feels excited, even privileged, like when he told her that she was famous. Another part is hostile, that he might be making assumptions about her. She is distracted from her thoughts as the car approaches her driveway.

Froyd leans forward and observes the huge house as the vehicle moves through the grounds towards the garage. "Wow! This is some pad."

The roller door raises, and Lilly drives the Bentley slowly inside. Hanging from the ceiling is a golf ball. She moves the car slowly forward until the ball just touches the windscreen. Then she shuts off the engine.

Froyd nods silently. Impressed with the precision.

Lilly leads him through the house, towards the kitchen. In the hallway, Froyd stops in front of a large display case that contains a collection of crockery that has been broken and then repaired with gold-coloured glue. “This is awesome,” Froyd says. “What is this?”

Lilly stands next to him, and says, proudly, “It’s called Kintsugi. Gold joinery. It’s an ancient Japanese art-form. It shows that things can be more beautiful repaired than before they were broken.”

“I like it,” says Froyd, impressed.

“This way.” Lilly leads him into the kitchen and points to a chair. “Sit.” She pours hot coffee from a pot into a large white cup with vibrant blue painting on the side, and places it in front of him. Then she takes a little tray containing milk, cream from the fridge and puts this alongside the cup.

“Thank you.”

“You just sit here.”

Lilly departs the kitchen for the bathroom in the larger of the spare rooms. When she returns, she is officious, like a grumpy nurse. She leads Froyd upstairs to the *ensuite* of the magnificent bedroom. The bathroom is tiled with marble, looking like something out of the aristocracy. The bath is huge, now filled with hot water and a thick coat of bubbles.

“Undress and throw your clothes out the door. It will take me an hour to turn them around. In the meantime, sit in there.” She points to the bubbles. “There is a bathrobe, towels, everything you need. There is a food platter, too.”

The platter is a collection of sweet meats and cheese, a bunch of grapes and slices of melon.

"Where's the minibar?" Froyd jests.

"It's right there," Lilly says, pointing. "Help yourself."

"There's a minibar in the bathroom?" Froyd laughs, shaking his head in disbelief. He steps inside the palatial room, and Lilly closes the door behind him.

Hours pass and Lilly is seated in her cocoon, browsing the Vita website and the two documents that Froyd had given her, the PB Checklist and the Planetary Death Spiral. Outside, the rain continues to fall heavily, making a muffled hiss. It is early evening, and the sky is dark.

Lilly sees movement reflected in the bay windows. She turns to see Froyd standing in the room. He is wearing the bathrobe and holding a crystal tumbler containing a gold-coloured spirit and big chunks of ice.

He says with a humble tone, "That bathtub is a most extraordinary thing. I feel better than I have in a very long time. Thank you, Lilly."

"You are welcome, Froyd. Sit down. Did you eat?"

"I did. Thank you."

"Did you see your clothes on the end of the bed?"

Froyd sits and adjusts the bathrobe. “I did. Thank you. I am enjoying this.” He motions towards the bathrobe.

“That’s Quitlan Mare. Very good brand.”

“I like your house, Lilly. You’ve got some great toys.”

“I am very fortunate to have nice things.”

“Do you live here alone?”

“I have been looking at your material. What is it all for?”

Froyd takes a sip of the whiskey and rolls it around his mouth. “I am trying to foster mass-Ecophany before we trigger the cascade of climate tipping points.”

“And what is that in English?”

“It’s a global spiritual awakening about the need for personal transformation in the face of the climate and ecological crisis. I am aiming to raise a global army of environmental warriors through a spiritual movement.”

Lilly thinks this through for a while. These are all foreign words and ideas to her. The climate crisis, as far as she can gather, is something that happens on youtube documentaries, or the evening news. It is very far away, and it certainly doesn’t happen to her. “And how do you intend to do that?” she asks.

“Shortly, I will finalise my plan and then enrol a

small group of people to implement it."

"*Uh-huh*? And who are these lucky people?"

"Well, that's you, Lilly. And your two sisters, Kara and Rae."

Lilly breaks into laughter. She looks at Froyd and sees that he is watching her, impassively, with a sly grin on his face. When she is able to draw breath, she says directly, "Well, that's not going to happen."

"You don't think so?"

"No!" The way that Lilly enunciates that single word is distinct, as the lioness rises to the fore again. Lilly Lord, for all her foibles, is a tough, capable woman who created a multi-million-dollar finance empire called Chartreuse Capital, in her thirties and has lived off its bounty ever since. One doesn't get to do that without having a means of communication that puts people squarely in their place when they step out of line.

Her tone is curt, downright scary even, as she says, "You know, Froyd Denison, I am okay that you are living in the neighbourhood. But to think that you are sitting in that house plotting things for my family and me; that is absolutely not okay. So, you need to start plotting something else instead. Do you understand?"

Froyd's facial reaction indicates that he has taken the message as it was intended: claws out. He nods slowly for a while, before he lowers his head and mutters, "It might be too late for that."

Lilly's wears a graven frown and she practically growls, "Then in the morning, I'll drop you at your front door, and you and I will have nothing more to do with each other."

Tom Cat Flies In

In the morning, the rain has ceased, and the sky is clear. Wearing her dressing gown, Lilly stands next to the window in her room, looking at the deadly roses. She is feeling uneasy, not knowing what woke her. Then she hears a familiar sound. It is distant but approaching rapidly. She peers through the window to the left, then the right, scanning the sky.

"Damn him!" she growls.

Just then, straight in front of her window, just thirty meters away, a black helicopter flashes past making a whining noise that reverberates through the room. Even through the triple glazing, it is possible to smell the exhaust gas. Lilly hates the smell of exhaust gas, particularly helicopter exhaust in her bedroom!

"Damn you, Tom Cata!" She sweeps out of her room, and down the stairs. As she rushes through the laundry towards the back door, she picks up a broom. In the yard, she marches into the downwash of the helicopter in her dressing gown and slippers, holding the broom handle high. The hot exhaust of the turbine engines washes over her, blasting through her hair.

Flying the chopper, Lilly's husband finds himself denied the opportunity to land in his normal spot, as a result of the serried ranks of area-denial rosebushes. He settles the chopper on the grass further down the yard, grumbling out loud. "Geeze! I am going to have to walk to the damned house. *Uh-oh!* Welcoming party."

He watches Lilly march towards the chopper with the broom and hears her banging on the fuselage with the wooden handle. "Oy! Watch the paintwork!" he yells out.

In the palatial bedroom, Froyd stands next to the window watching battle of wills take place in the yard. The mornings are always hard, and he props himself against the wall, his coughing fit interrupted by laughter. It makes him lightheaded and he crawls back onto the bed, exhausted.

Lilly's husband, Tom, steps out of the chopper. He is a solid, well-fed man wearing suit pants, white silk shirt and red braces. He opens his arms and walks towards Lilly, "Come and give your old man a kiss." He forces his mouth on her cheek and grabs her ass.

"Get off me, Tom!" She breaks free and storms towards the house.

"Kitten?" he calls out. "Tom Cat's bought a present."

"Shove it up your ass, Tom!" Lilly shouts, over her shoulder.

Tom returns to the helicopter to retrieve his briefcase and a bottle of wine, and then follows her inside. He moves around the house, calling out, "Where's my little kitty kitty? Tom Cat's coming for you."

She's in the kitchen, facing the bench, grinding her teeth. Tom approaches and places his hand on her waist.

Lilly turns on him, "Don't think that you can just fly in here on a booty call. I'm not your damned whore!"

"Settle, Lilly, settle. I come bearing gifts." Tom holds up a bottle of *Reserva Carménere,* a red wine from the Pinto Bendeira district of Brazil. The mere sight of the bottle - her favourite wine, and the only red that Lilly drinks - makes her bold, and she reaches for it, instinctively.

"*Uh, uh, uh,*" Tom taunts, moving the wine out her reach. "Not until you say…"

She shakes her head, not interested in following through on the ritual. She can't hold out for long before a smile breaks. "You are a man of intensity and identity, like the wine itself," Lilly says coldly.

Tom passes over the bottle. "The day that you start buying this online, I will lose my hold on you, forever."

"It just wouldn't be the same though, would it?" Lilly places the wine out of view, and becomes frosty, again. "I haven't heard from you for months, then you just decide to show up, unannounced."

"I know. I know. I should have called. But there's pressing business to discuss."

This defuses the tension somewhat. "You want some coffee?"

"I'd love some coffee."

"So where have you been?"

"Oh, you know, around? South America. North America."

"And what are you doing here?" Lilly asks, flatly.

"Chartreuse Capital has its annual general meeting coming up and I have a bold new plan. I wanted to strategize with my co-Director."

"*Uh-huh.*" Lilly places a cup on the table in front of Tom, the same Jumbo Spode cup that she served Froyd with the night before. She pours the black coffee from the pot, and then slides the cup towards him.

Now, if Tom had answered her question by saying that he was visiting because he wanted to spend some time with her, she would have included milk, cream, sugar, and maybe even some biscuits.

"What's on your mind, then?" she crosses her arms.

Tom glances around the room, hoping to see something to sweeten the coffee. That's just not going to happen, it seems. "I've been in the States looking at their shale operations. There's a lot of money in it, and it's all finance driven. I want to make a play for shale in Australia."

"I don't know anything about shale," Lilly says.

"Fracking," Tom says, using his hands for emphasis. "It's all in the news."

"Fracking?" Lilly is suddenly reminded that Froyd Denison is in the house. "You mean using fracking fluid?" She glances towards the door; anxiously thinking that Froyd might be there, listening in. He's not, thankfully. But if he were, how would she explain his presence to Tom? She suddenly feels exposed. Fortunately, Tom is distracted.

"Who the f*** is that?" he suddenly says, pointing through the window.

Lilly turns to see, down the yard beyond the rose bushes, Froyd is standing there, looking at the helicopter. He is dressed in the clothes that she washed for him last night.

Tom rushes out of the kitchen and Lilly puts her hand against her mouth, unable to contain the surprise. "Oh, dear. This could get messy."

Then her attention is drawn to Tom's smartphone on the bench top. Casually, she picks it up and types in the passcode. She knows the passcode because she has coyly observed him enter it numerous times in the past. This, however, is the first time that she has had the opportunity to use that knowledge. She opens the app that shows the photos. True to his word, he is pictured standing with North American men in a paddock. She flicks through picture after picture of shale projects; dirty twisted pipes, sooty vehicles and red-necked workers. Formerly abundant landscapes now poisoned by the toxic, industrial process.

Then the photos take her to South America, but not for shale business, something very different: nightclubs, strip-bars and brothels. There is a picture of Tom dancing with a practically naked young woman. The subsequent photos show Tom undressing, and then screwing, said woman.

Tom's infidelity is no surprise to Lilly, but the clarity of the photos is! Better yet, the photos have a time and date stamp on them.

"Got you, Tom Cat."

On the lawn, Tom Cata bowls up to Froyd Denison, barking abuse that ends with, "Who the hell are you?"

"G'day," says Froyd with a friendly smile. "This your chopper?"

"What the f*** are you doing here?"

"I'm just looking for the fuel cap, mate. Where is it?"

"What?"

"Where am I supposed to put the sugar in."

Lilly glances up to see the altercation, intrigued by the body language as Froyd and Tom engage in conversation. It goes through a couple of different phases. At first, Tom is animated, then he listens intently, and then he looks towards the house, nodding.

Lilly opens the email app on Tom's phone and sends the most salacious photos to herself, using an email address that doesn't disclose her identity. Then she deletes the record of the sent email. Lilly places the phone on the table, and then goes to the window to watch the action.

"What on Earth is going on?" Lilly asks aloud, watching Tom moving quickly in her direction.

He enters the kitchen hurriedly. He is panting and his eyes dart furtively around the bench tops. He grabs his phone and his briefcase and just before he departs, he mutters, "We'll talk about this later."

Tom storms down the yard, past the rose bushes, towards the helicopter. And then, to Lilly's complete surprise, both he and Froyd step into the chopper. The engines roar into life, the rotors start to spin, the craft lifts off the grass, turns in the air, and then disappears from view.

Lilly is stunned, unable to make any sense of any of it. She rests her back against the bench. Her heart and her mind are pounding trying to cognitively and emotionally make sense of what just happened. She feels her face flush red and her breathing adjust to short sharp bursts. It's a panick attack, and she needs something to break through. She casts her eyes around the room, looking for something.

On the table is the porcelain cup containing Tom's undrunk black coffee. She empties the cup into the sink, rinses it, dries it, and places it very delicately on the cupboard so that it is half hanging over the edge in such a manner that the faintest movement will see it fall.

Then she opens the cupboard door to its full extent, releases it, and steps back, folding her arms.

The cupboard door closes slowly right to near the end, and then pauses momentarily before snapping shut. The motion of the door hitting the frame is all that is needed to dislodge the Spode cup.

The cup falls, hits the tiles, and smashes into pieces. The sound is a deeply satisfying clatter followed by multiple skittering noises as the smashed crockery slides across the tiles.

Lilly stands in her place, reliving the motion and the sound of the shattering cup, playing it over and over in her mind. It has a cathartic effect, and she sighs. How awesome it is that something so beautiful and valuable can be reduced to useless pieces of china with such a subtle movement as a cupboard door closing. How vulnerable are even the beautiful and the expensive things, she thinks. How easy is it to destroy that which is revered? She inhales at length, and then exhales slowly. It is over.

Lilly takes the *Reserva Carménere* to her cocoon. Seated in her chair that overlooks the recently demonstrated helicopter denying rose bushes, she sends a text to her housemaid instructing her to pick up the pieces of broken china from the kitchen floor and to send them to the Kintsugi factory as soon as possible. Then she sends a text message to Vinnie that simply reads: "Have I got news for you?"

Debriefing Vinnie

As it happens, Vinnie also has news for Lilly. The private eye has come back with another sheaf of information, deepening the mystery of Froyd Denison even further. Over another long lunch in the restaurant on the jetty in Church Point, Lilly discloses her previous twenty-four hours.

She explains how she had most firmly put Froyd Denison in his place, only to have him fly off in her philandering husband's helicopter the morning after, with not so much as a 'by your leave'.

"I can't believe his audacity," says Vinnie, visibly shocked. "What was he talking to Tom about?"

"I have no idea."

"Do you think that they know each other?"

"No."

"You don't think that maybe..?"

"What?" Lilly glares at Vinnie. Without words, she communicates in no uncertain terms that there is to be no consideration that Tom Cata is Froyd Denison's missing father.

Vinnie picks up on the cold vibe immediately, and changes tack. "It makes no sense," she says, perplexed.

"You know, Vinnie, it seems the more that I know about Froyd Denison, the less I know about Froyd Denison."

"Well, this should help," Vinnie taps a fingernail on the envelope containing the latest Denison intelligence. "After you've digested this lot, you'll know almost nothing at all."

"I wish," sighs Lilly. "It's exhausting. Just thinking about him plotting things for me. It's plain creepy."

"You and your sisters."

"Even worse."

"Didn't you say that Rae was running an event soon?"

"Yes. I'm thinking I might go there and warn her."

"Well, count me in. Even though it won't be catered. And what about Kara? Where's Kara these days."

"She's still touring capital cities doing her Happiness show." Lilly sighs. "So, what's the new information?"

Vinnie opens the folder and shifts the documents around as she speaks. "Well, we know that Mrs Denison passed-on recently. Complications associated with alcohol addiction."

"Oh, really?" asks Lilly, placing her wine glass on the coaster and pushing it a few inches across the table.

"Cask wine, apparently." Vinnie leans forward

and whispers conspiratorially, "Coolabah Riesling."

"Well, that would explain it," Lilly says. She retrieves the chilled Chablis from the ice bucket and adds a dash into her glass.

"Apparently, she was a hoarder. The spare room was filled with empty boxes."

"Well, that's a fire hazard."

"Froyd was with her when she died."

"And what about the will and the property?"

"The P.I. is still working on that."

Vinnie reaches for the Chablis and sees that the bottle is nearly empty. She turns in her seat to look for the waiter. She sees the same young waiter who she tormented last time she was in the restaurant. He is adjusting cutlery on one of the tables, not looking in her direction. Vinnie hisses at him, "Oy!"

Startled, the young waiter scurries over, full of apologies. "I'm sorry, Miss." He retrieves his note pad, fumbles and drops it on the ground. He leans down to retrieve it and bumps his head on the table on the way up, making the cutlery jangle.

Vinnie pressures him with her scorn. "Listen here, boy. Get your shit together, or I'll have you fired."

"Yes, Miss," he trembles.

"Get me another one of these," she waggles the Chablis bottle.

"Yes. Miss." He turns to move away.

" And waiter!"

He returns, an anxious look on his face. "Yes, Miss."

"It's Ms."

"Yes, Miss, thank you."

"Right," says Vinnie, content that her sadistic ritual has been fulfilled. "Where were we?"

"Rae," Lilly says. "We are going to see Rae."

The Transition Event

Rae's event is held in a lecture hall in a Sydney university. The auditorium is filled with three hundred people seated and another fifty or so standing in the aisles.

Lilly and Vinnie are seated in the back row. Lilly scans the crowd with her antique theatre glasses, while Vinnie complains, "It's hardly the Opera House, is it?"

Lilly directs the glasses onto the podium as her sister Rae, steps up. She adjusts some documents and then looks up and see's Lilly spying on her.

"Hi Lilly," Rae waves. "It's my elder sister, up the back." Hundreds of people crane their necks around to look in Lilly's direction. Lilly lowers the glasses, embarrassed. She feebly raises a hand to wave at them, not impressed to be in the spotlight.

"How embarrassing," Vinnie hisses.

"Tell me about it."

"I can't believe that she *ad-libbed* like that."

"She was always speaking out of turn."

Rae proceeds with her presentation and about half-way through, Vinnie loses concentration. "What's she even talking about?"

"She says we shouldn't use coal anymore."

"Why not?"

"It makes the weather change, you see."

"You want to nip that in the bud. Half of your share portfolio is coal, isn't it?"

"A lot of it, yes."

"It all just means trouble as far as I'm concerned."

After the event, Vinnie is edgy, anxious to get underway, but Lilly halts her. Rae appears, surrounded by a group of supporters.

"I am going to get us a wine. Go and talk to your sister." Vinnie moves over to the makeshift table where volunteers are serving drinks and nibbles.

A young woman of about twenty wearing a blue shirt with a white circular logo says, "Hi."

"Two Sav Blancs."

"We have only white or red."

"Two whites, then."

"That's four dollars, thanks." She pours the wine into a paper coffee cup.

"That's quaint. You don't use wine glasses?"

"This is better than glass. They are compostable, you see."

Vinnie retrieves an American Express card from her clutch and points it at the volunteer. "What? You don't have eftpos?"

"It's not really like that. The wine is donated by members, you see. You should probably just have these," the volunteer hands over the cups.

"What a strange arrangement," Vinnie mumbles. She sniffs the edge of the cup and mumbles, "It's overpriced." She sees that Lilly is talking with Rae.

"It's so lovely to see you," Rae says, holding her elder sister's hand.

"Have you got a minute for me?" Lilly asks.

"Of course I have."

Rae escorts Lilly to an office and closes the door behind her. "It's so nice to see you, Lilly," Rae takes her hands again.

"You too. I have really left it so long."

"We've both got busy lives, I guess."

"You got a good crowd here tonight."

"Not big enough to change the world, though."

"It'll happen," Lilly says.

"Do you think so? It's funny to see you here. The Queen of Coal is a closet environmentalist?" Rae taunts.

"I never did like that title."

"So, what brings you here?"

"I have been having some conversations with a man called Froyd Denison."

"Froyd Denison?" Rae asks, surprised.

"You know him?"

"Yes. I know Froyd."

"How do you know him?"

"He's a bit of a hero in these circles." Rae cocks her head, confused. "How did you meet Froyd?"

"He's living near me now. I keep bumping into him."

"Well, it sounds like he's having a good effect on you."

"It's actually rather spooky." Lilly glances around, to check that they are alone. She lowers her voice and says, conspiratorially. "He says that he has a grand plan for my life. And it involves you and Kara."

Rae laughs aloud. "Awesome. That definitely sounds like Froyd. So, what's the plan?"

"I haven't given him the space to tell me yet."

"Well, when you find out, I'd love to know. He's really very bright. Look I really must get back to wrap up. Can I see you afterwards?"

"No, I'll go now. But let's catch up soon. So much to talk about."

Fukushima Ling

After dropping Vinnie off at home, Lilly drives to the corner of Roberts Road and pulls up on the gravel. She sits there for some time with the engine running, wondering what to do next. One part of her wants to berate Froyd for having a plan for her life; another part wants to know what the plan is. The brief discussion with Rae had gone some way to easing her fears, and raising her curiosity about Froyd's intent.

After ten minutes on the side of the road stuck in indecision, she decides to tempt fate by reconnoitring. So, she drives down the dirt road, past Froyd's driveway. She continues a way down the road before doing a U-turn and driving back.

At the last moment, she turns into the driveway, pulling up next to the front room. With the engine running she watches for movement in the curtains.

Eventually, the curtain is shifted aside and Froyd's face appears in the window. He looks exhausted, dark rings under his eyes. He nods slowly, then ushers Lilly to come inside. He meets her in the hallway. "Have you got any booze?"

"Is that the best thing for you?"

"Humour me, Lilly. Would you, please?"

"I'll see what I can find." Lilly goes to the car, pops the boot, and rummages around in a large picnic hamper. Minutes later she returns with a small bottle of schnapps.

She hands Froyd the bottle, and he appreciatively removes the lid, and takes a swig. He grimaces as the alcohol slides down his throat. "The worst thing is the taste in my mouth," he tells her.

"From the frack fluid?"

"Radiation poisoning."

"Where did you get radiation poisoning?"

"Oh, on my travels. You know."

Lilly makes to sit, but the spare chair is covered in documents.

"Just throw that shit on the floor," Froyd instructs her.

Lilly tidies the documents into a pile, and places them on the carpet. She sits and asks, "So, where did you go on your holiday?"

Froyd rests back in his seat, settling him. "A few years back I took a trip to Borneo, the Aral Sea, the Citarum River and Fukushima."

"I've never heard of those places."

"Yeah," Froyd chuckles, "Flight Centre doesn't do specials to those places. It was a tour of ecological hot spots. I went to see the cut forests, the empty lakes, the waterway that is more plastic than water and the irradiated coastline."

"Why?"

"I wanted to see for myself what the ecological death of a planet looks like."

"That's a bit melodramatic, isn't it?"

Froyd sips some more schnapps. He sits back in his chair observing Lilly with a displeased look. Eventually, he says, "No."

"No? No, what?"

"No, it's not melodramatic. It is a matter of fact. Our biosphere is dying." He sits forward, saying, "I know that is esoteric language. Let me use an analogy."

"Okay."

"Consider a new car, fresh out of the showroom. Everything works. It's unblemished. Can you picture that?"

"I can."

"So, lets give the keys to an undisciplined teenager who lives in the bush. First, there is exceptional wear and tear, and dirt builds up that doesn't get cleaned away. Then a scratch in the paintwork and the metal gets exposed and oxidation starts. Then the electric window fails and the rain gets in. That makes the inside of the car smell. On and on it goes, month after month, year after year. You can imagine this?"

"Yes. The car is falling apart."

"That's right. The car's got bits hanging off it, but

it still runs. And the shittier the car gets, the less respect it gets, so the atrophy accelerates. Eventually, it's like one of those bush cars with a piece of wire for the accelerator and a pair of monkey grips for a steering wheel, blowing smoke, all flat tyres, but somehow still driving. Then one day, it just stops working and it can't be started again. It gets abandoned by the roadside and maybe one day, years later, gets picked up for scrap metal and a few spare parts."

"Okay, I get that," says Lilly. "So, what does it mean?"

"Well, the car is our global ecosystem, Lilly – the skin of our Living Planet. And the irresponsible teenager driving it, that's the humans. But the people who live in the bubble world don't see that."

Lilly looks around the dilapidated house. She's not convinced.

Froyd picks up on it. "No?"

"I am not sure of your perspective."

"My perspective? That's funny."

"Why is that funny?"

"I am of the millennial generation. And you are a baby-boomer. And you are telling me that my perspective is off. That's ripe!"

"What has generations got to do with it?"

"Everything, Lilly. Everything. Your generation

has sucked all the goodness out of this planet and left my generation with shit. You've gutted the natural capital and turned it into cash for your investment portfolios. You've left us with a depleted planet that's choked with millions of tons of plastic shit, just waiting for a mega-storm to send it into the ocean. Your generation has turned this planet into 'an immense pile of filth' – and I'm quoting the Pope, now. And now you sit at home, in your country clubs, behind your security gates, blaming the poor for being angry. Let me quote from written text."

"Must you?"

"It's obligatory that you to hear this at least once." Froyd pulls his laptop on to his knees and searches for a file. He paraphrases the first section, then the reads the rest verbatim.

"So, we start with a list of the Planetary Boundaries that have been smashed through by the Baby-boomers: climate change, biodiversity, forty percent of the phytoplankton killed off, all that stuff. And then… Despite these extraordinary statistics, the best that the aged ruling class can suggest is minor variations of the very same Business as Usual that got us here in the first place. And so, the ecodical madness continues unabated, getting deeper and more intractable every day."

Froyd glances up to see that Lilly is still

concentrating. She nods her head grimly; so, he continues.

"The young generation once looked up to the elder generation for wisdom and advice. Today, what the young see when they look up is the elders luxuriating on their balconies, protected from the surface-dwellers by security fences. While the young live with the consequences of a dying planet, the old live it up in style."

"Never in human history, has a generation gotten so rich by stealing so much from its offspring's future. For the first time in history, an entire younger generation has been denied a birth-right. Instead, they've been left a birth-debt, and no means to pay it."

"Okay. Okay." Lilly holds up her hand, overwhelmed by Froyd's invective. She fans herself, feeling light-headed. "Oh, boy," she bites back. "You're an angry ant today, aren't you?"

Froyd chuckles and makes himself comfy in his chair. He swigs on the schnapps, rolling the fluid around in his mouth. "Thanks for the schnapps, hey. I feel much better."

"What was that? An essay for *Spite Weekly*?"

"*Nahh.* It's just me blowing off steam." He slides the laptop down the side of the cushion. "So, Lilly. You clearly didn't come here to hear my philosophy on baby-boomers. So, what did you come here for?"

"I came here to say that whatever it is you are planning, don't plan it for me. It's nothing to do with me."

"It's everything to do with you, Lilly. That's the point that you people don't get. Your mob caused it, and my mob will suffer it, but we're all in this together. Where do you think we are all going to go in a world that is two degrees above baseline? When the phytoplankton is washing up dead on the beach. It's all hands on deck, Lilly. And because you haven't figured it out for yourself, I have done it for you."

"Oh, boy, you're audacious."

"Aren't you curious about your mission?"

"Okay, Froyd," Lilly says, defiantly. "Why don't you entertain me with your plan for my life?"

"Good. Are you ready?"

"Sure."

"You are going to put together a program that fosters mass-Ecophany. It starts in this country and spreads around the world. You, Lilly, will launch a global, spiritual revolution for sustainability. And you will do this with ease, and be happy and fulfilled to be have done so."

"I think that you and I have different definitions of sustainability."

Froyd fixes her with a stern look, "Let's just stick to my version, shall we? You're the Queen of Coal, remember. This is my field of expertise, not yours. You remember the analogy about the car?"

"Yes. The abused car."

"Well, this planet is like the car with the wire for the accelerator and the spanner for a steering wheel. It is on the verge of becoming un-driveable. We have to get off fossil fuels A.S.A.P., and regrow natural capital, change the world's diet, materials and energy supplies. We need to do this as a matter of urgency. A war-footing. Sun Tzu. von Clausewitz. Manhattan Project. Throw everything at it. We need to light a fuse under the public so that they stop voting for imbeciles and wasting time and money on things that don't achieve these aims."

"And how am I supposed to do that?"

"I have designed a program for you."

"A program?"

"Chrysalis Day."

"What?"

"The program is called Chrysalis Day."

"Chrysalis Day?" The words immediately capture Lilly's attention. They conjure images of a cocoon with a caterpillar squirming inside, undergoing transformation. Changing, becoming unrecognisable from its previous form. And on a particular day; is that just one day, or are there multiple Chrysalis Days? How many Chrysalis Days can one have? Lilly finds herself falling into a rabbit hole of wonder at the idea of Chrysalis Day, not even knowing what it is. "Chrysalis Day," she says again. "Tell me about it."

Froyd retrieves a manila envelope from the side of the seat. He holds it out towards Lilly.

"And what's that?"

"It details what you and your sisters need to do."

"My sisters?"

"It's a draft, for your consideration. I'll have it complete shortly." He continues to hold it out, but Lilly makes no effort to retrieve it from him. He drops it onto the floor in front of her.

Lilly goes silent. She looks around the room, astounded at the idea. Her mind is a tangle of thoughts. Her sisters?

"You've got my life all sorted out, haven't you?"

"Sometimes, we need direction."

"*Uh-huh*? And what makes you think my life needs direction?"

"Your rose bushes."

Froyd's words take Lilly by surprise. She is struck by how quickly he responded, and how vulnerable she feels on hearing them. For a second, she considers arguing with him, but she doesn't feel herself to be on solid ground to do that. Instead, she deflects and asks, "And why don't you run the show?"

"Because I'll be dead soon."

"What does that mean?"

"It means that I am going to be dead, soon."

"Dead?" Lilly laughs. "You almost said that like you meant it."

Froyd clears his throat and adjusts his position on the chair. "I mentioned that I went to Fukushima in my travels."

Lilly shrugs.

"It's not a luxury resort, Lilly. It's a province in Japan that was hit by a tsunami."

"And what's that?"

"A huge wave caused by an underwater earthquake. This was in 2011. Anyway, there was a nuclear power station there, Fukushima Daiichi. It was seriously damaged."

"That's not a good thing, I assume."

"It's a terrible mess; to this day, even. Three reactors melted down and there's a mass of corium, pouring radiation into the Pacific Ocean. The Japanese Prime Minister was contemplating evacuating Tokyo - that's thirty million people – can you imagine that?"

"Why are you telling me this?"

"Because I went there, to Fukushima, on my travels. They evacuated the region because of all of the radioactive fallout. They abandoned homes, schools, and hospitals. And a zoo."

"You went to the zoo?"

"Correct."

"Why?"

"In this zoo, there was an exhibit of the Black Ling, it's a type of fish. It's extinct in the wild, and the only place in the world it lives, is in that abandoned aquarium. And with no power, no light, no one to feed it, they were going to die, unless someone intervened. And if they died, then the species died. You've heard of the Sixth Extinction?"

"I watched a video, but I don't know any of this stuff, Froyd."

"Well, in our geological past, there have been five mass extinction events, when most of the species were killed off through natural processes. The humans are now creating the sixth. Stopping the Black Ling going extinct would slow that down a bit. Just a tiny bit. But what else ought we do with our lives, Lilly? Sustainability and happiness, remember?"

"So, you went to a zoo in a nuclear disaster zone to free a fish," Lilly shakes her head, astounded.

"There were eight fish, and there were four of us. And it wasn't just eight fish, it was the last eight fish. Big difference."

"And what happened?"

"Well, we got in okay. It just took us forever to get out."

"Why?"

"Proper preparation prevents piss poor performance, Lilly. We didn't plan it properly. For example, the picture we had of the fish was really old, and when we got there, the fish were much bigger," Froyd chuckles as he recalls the day. "They were huge. We thought that we were going in for minnows. These things were like baby whales," he indicates with his hands. "So, we needed to transport them with about a tonne of water. So, we needed to find an appropriate container. We needed to find a truck and a forklift. It just went on forever."

"Did you get the fish out?"

"Eventually. We hooked up with some marine scientists and we released them on the coast where they had a chance of survival."

"And did they survive?"

"Don't know. Maybe. Maybe not." Froyd looks down at his hands, and sighs. He sits back, his body slumps, exhausted from telling the story. He takes a long swig of Schnapps and this enlivens him.

Lilly sits back in her chair, thinking over the story. "All that radioactivity must have been bad for your health."

"That's right. We all got a lot more radiation than we had planned. The others were okay, but I copped a full load. I got a hot pebble stuck in my shoe and it flooded me with gamma rays and alpha particles. That's what kicked off the blood cancer."

"You have blood cancer?"

"When it was diagnosed, I was told I had six months."

"How long ago was that?"

"About three months ago. About when my mother died."

"And what about the frack fluid?"

"Well, slipping into a drum of frack fluid didn't improve my health. But I was the expendable one, right?"

"Are you getting treatment?"

"It's not one you treat, Lilly. It's all through the marrow. It's growing every day. I can feel it. The weakness. The pain. It's there, in the background, waiting to pounce. Except that I'm not going to let it."

"What are you going to do?"

"Live life fully until it is time to die. Friday week."

"What happens Friday week?"

"That's when I shuffle off this mortal coil, back into the flux."

"You're very specific about the day."

"Unlike the trip to Fukushima, this is well planned."

"What, did you just throw a dart at a calendar?" Lilly chuckles at her own joke.

"When I made the decision, I figured the date would be about three months away, so that gave me the week. I'd get to the end of the week, throw a party with my friends, then slip off shortly after that."

"You're going to kill yourself?" Lilly gasps.

"Correct."

"Well, you can't do that."

"I have just told you that I can do that."

"What are you going to do?"

"I am going to sit in the waterhole in the creek, out the back here, and bleed out quietly through my arms."

"You are going to cut your wrists?"

"No, Lilly!" Froyd shakes his head, annoyed at her tone. "I'll use proper medical equipment. A cannula. I'll drink some wine, take some paprika, get merry, and when the time is right, open the taps."

"And then you'll just rot in the river?"

Froyd inhales deeply. He studies Lilly, noting how beautifully presented she is; the fibres of her clothes, the jewellery, her hair and makeup. It's like a fine artist has designed her. Sure, she looks lovely. But that brain of hers needs to be seriously rewired. "Is it the same with all the Baby-boomers?" he wonders.

"It's all planned," Froyd says, tersely. "The medics will come and get me. No one has to be disturbed by my passing."

"Except for you."

"You're not listening, Lilly. I am avoiding pain."

"Well, I think that you are crazy, and you ought to be locked up." She stands, holding her handbag to her chest.

"Think about that for a minute. You want to deprive me of liberty, stop me living life the way I want to live it. And you think that is humane; somehow noble? Are you serious?"

Lilly moves her hand to indicate the dilapidated house with science papers scattered all around. "Is this really how you want to live your life?" she asks, disdainfully.

"No, Lilly. This is how I want to live my life," Froyd moves his finger back and forward between them. "This conversation is how I want to live my life. Honest, non-infantile, Big Talk. Leaving something extraordinary for after I am gone."

"Then why kill yourself ahead of time."

"I intend to die with blood cancer, not of it. I'll go my way, in my own time. And I want to fill my days up ahead of then. I want to teach you what you need to do."

Lilly takes a step towards the door. "Well, count me out of it. You need to be on medication." She taps the side of her head with a finger. "It's an interesting story, Froyd. Assuming that it's true. But I don't want to be part of it. Sorry."

"You are already a part of."

"In your mind, maybe. I don't have time for these riddles." Lilly departs the room.

Froyd heaves a sigh and listens to the sound of the vehicle exiting the driveway. He raises the bottle to the empty room. "Thanks for the schnapps."

Golf Ball & Kintsugi

When Lilly arrives home, she is driving faster than normal and finds herself having to wait for the garage door to open. The delay is interminable, and she starts to think about how annoying Froyd Denison is. How is it that someone who doesn't even live with mains electricity or hot water has the temerity to give her life instructions. And how annoying is it that she is annoyed by him?

Finally, the garage door is open and she drives the vehicle inside. Rather than gently moving up against the suspended golf ball, she allows the vehicle to roll further forward that it ought before jamming on the brakes. The windscreen smacks into the golf ball forcing it forward. It returns at speed and bangs against the glass, bouncing off. And so it goes, bouncing back and forth, rapping against the glass, the length of its swing reducing, and the speed of its movement increasing, until it lets out a death rattle that makes a distinctive *B-R-R-R-R-R-T!* noise and then comes to a rest.

The effect is mesmerizing, and Lilly sits there, her eyes locked on the stationary white ball. Finally, she steps out of the car, still not quite straight with the world. In front of the Kintsugi cabinet, she halts, and a thought occurs to her.

She opens the cabinet, retrieves one of the repaired plates, takes it into the kitchen, and places it very delicately on the edge of the cupboard. As she opens the cupboard door, she feels a pang of doubt, unsure whether it is right to smash and then repair something that has already been smashed and then repaired. Nonetheless, she lets the door go free and steps back to watch her handy work. The door swings closed, and then pauses just for a few moments. In that brief time, Lilly has second thoughts and she panics. She lashes her hand out to prevent the door from closing but in so doing, bumps up against the cupboard, causing the plate to slip. She darts out her hand to catch it, but is unable to grasp the plate, instead bumping it so that it's fall is now imparted with spin.

When the plate strikes the tiles, it explodes into a thousand pieces with a brittle crunching noise. The pieces fly not just horizontally across the floor, but up in the air.

The effect is awesome and the noise of the pieces falling to the tiled floor is hugely gratifying. Lilly slumps on the floor, and starts to laugh so intensely, that it brings tears to her eyes.

Visiting Chartreuse Capital

The next morning, Lilly drives the black Mercedes to North Sydney, where the offices of Chartreuse Capital are located. The corporate headquarters of the hedge fund are suitably opulent; the decor characterised by stainless steel and tinted glass. There is a cabinet display of Kintsugi - $20,000 worth of smashed Spode and Wedgewood - a reminder of the exasperation that had been associated with creating the company on her own, all those years ago.

Lilly had worked hard to create Chartreuse Capital, and had committed a lot of her own money to kick it off. Today, however, she has negligible involvement in the company; she keeps a minimal amount of Chartreuse documentation at home and attends only the annual and extra-ordinary board meetings. Her hands-off approach is based on an early agreement with Tom; she would fund and establish the company, and he would run it. The agreement has worked well for over twenty years. Tom, in his role as Chairman, oversees the board and the Chief Executive, and ensures that the money keeps rolling in.

After a briefing from the CEO, Lilly spends the morning in the boardroom reading through the minutes of the previous board meetings, and the company financials.

By 1 pm, she is satisfied that she has the measure of the firm. She drives across the Sydney Harbour Bridge to Café Sydney, a prestigious restaurant on the rooftop of Customs House. The restaurant offers a spectacular view over the Circular Quay, the busy ferry terminal, and the Harbour Bridge.

Lilly applies the same intense concentration to the menu and wine list, as she had applied to the Chartreuse Capital documentation. Finally, she settles on the grilled swordfish with artichokes, and a glass of Mount Mary Chardonnay from the Yarra Valley, Victoria.

After her meal, she orders another wine, and checks her smartphone for messages from Vinnie. There are none. She sits back in her chair, sipping her drink, looking at Sydney Harbour, and thinking about Froyd Denison. She is wondering what he is doing, and whether he is still plotting things for her life.

After lunch, Lilly drives to Double Bay and spends a few hours browsing and window-shopping. She makes a few purchases including a piece of Korean crockery that she thinks will make an excellent addition to the Kintsugi cabinet, should the need ever arise.

Lilly feels at home in this up-market retail precinct. The streets are lined with prestigious motor vehicles, and the women are dressed in the latest fashion, with fascinators and high heels. In this place, Lilly feels a strong sense that everything is well in the world. This is despite that fact that the planet is more than one degree hotter than it ought to be, and that 50% of the world's wildlife has been wiped-out because humans behave like unsustainable super predators. You just wouldn't pick that up, window-shopping in Double Bay.

Lilly engages in a conversation with a woman in a fashion shop and doesn't even mention that she got negative six on the Planetary Boundaries checklist for the smaller of her three cars.

On the way out of Double Bay, Lilly drives past one of her properties, an Art Deco-styled apartment block that overlooks the harbour. The penthouse was her home when she was working in the city, setting up Chartreuse Capital. It has been mostly empty, ever since.

Lilly turns the vehicle around and pulls up across the road. She sends an angry text message to the property manager, notifying them that the hedges are overgrown. With that duty taken care of, she drives home to Duffys Forest.

Documentary Evidence

When Lilly pulls into her gate, she doesn't notice that Froyd is waiting for her, across the road, slumped against a tree. A few minutes after the gate has closed behind her, Froyd crosses the road. He presses the button on the intercom and rests his head against the wall, drained of energy.

After a while, the intercom crackles and Lilly addresses him, "What are you doing here?"

"I have something that you need to see." Froyd holds up a memory stick in front of the camera.

Inside the house, Lilly squints at the monitor, trying to make out what Froyd is holding. "Can't it wait?" she asks.

"No."

"Why not?"

"I am going away soon."

Lilly sighs, she is in no mood for Froyd Denison right now. She says nothing, hoping that he will just go away. However, when she sees Froyd move away from the intercom and out of sight of the camera, she panics, desperate for him to return. She presses the button to unlock the gate and waits anxiously, watching the monitor. Seconds tick by, and then Froyd comes back into view. He looks up at the camera, shaking his head, and wearing a stern look.

Lilly paces around the kitchen anxiously as she waits for him to reach the house. Finally, she hears the chimes, a distinguished sound of tubular bells, and walks quickly to the front door. She ushers Froyd into the kitchen and points to a stool, saying, "Sit."

Froyd chuckles and complies. Lilly opens the fridge that is bulging with fine product from all over the world. She retrieves a French ginger-beer, removes the lid and places it on a serviette next to a glass with ice.

Froyd pours the ginger beer and takes a sip. "That's delicious. Thank you."

Lilly rests back against the workstation, her arms crossed, glaring at him. "After our conversation the other day, I was very angry with you."

"*Uh-huh*? Are you still angry with me?"

"Yes, I am."

"And how's that working for you?" Froyd places the glass gently onto the place mat.

"It seems appropriate under the circumstances."

"Stick with it then."

"Who do you really think you are, that you can dictate to me how I ought to live my life?"

"I guess I hit a raw nerve, *huh*?"

"Your audacity offended me."

"I've written it down." Froyd retrieves from his

jacket pocket a white envelope. "*Oops!* Not that one." He pushes it back into his pocket, and then checks the other side. "Here you go." He slides a manila folder across the table towards her. It's been folded in half in his pocket, and he straightens it out flat.

"What's that?"

"That's the program that you'll be running with your sisters, when I am gone. Chrysalis Day, the final draft."

Lilly laughs, "Boy, you are persistent."

"Just indulge me for a little while, Lilly."

She moves the document across the table. "Just out of interest, Froyd, what is the budget for this project?"

"About a hundred million dollars."

Lilly coughs with disbelief. "Really?"

"That's the global program, commensurate to the scale of the sustainability crisis the world faces."

"So, you thought you'd find a wealthy woman to bankroll your project."

"Not just any wealthy woman. This program is designed specifically for Lillian Lord, the Queen of Coal."

"Don't call me that."

"It was on the cover of Business Review Weekly."

"That's not the point. And what makes you think

that I am the best athlete for this project?"

"I know your work."

"And how so?"

"I studied finance. You were my case study. I wrote a paper: *One Strong Woman: The Founding of Chartreuse Capital*. I got a High Distinction for it. I'll send you a copy, if you like."

"Well, if you think that I am going to use my money to fund your cause, you really are quite deluded."

"You haven't read the document, so I understand why you'd think that," Froyd says. "The program doesn't involve using your money, Lilly."

"*Uh-huh*? So, where's the money coming from?"

"It's your husband's money."

Lilly starts to laugh again. "Froyd, I entertain your youthful enthusiasms because I am quite partial to your company, prickly as it is. Actually, I do like you; you have bought mystery and excitement to my life."

"You are very welcome, Lilly."

"Good. Thank you. But my husband is not the charitable type. He is a selfish, greedy bastard. A real prick, actually. And I am certainly not going to ask him on your behalf. Really, your motive is noble, but your plan is completely misguided. It's not well thought through. You need to rethink it."

"Okay. Lilly. I hear you," Froyd says, calmly. "And thank you for being candid with me."

"You're most welcome."

"But you are wrong on two points."

"And what are they?"

"This is very well thought through. And I actually have two motives, not one."

"I'm listening," Lilly crosses her arms.

"One motive is noble; protecting Earth's living systems for the Long Future and promoting happiness world-wide. The other, less so."

"And what is your ignoble motive, Froyd?"

"Revenge."

"Revenge?" Lilly asks, intrigued. She thinks of Vinnie, wishing that here girlfriend was here to listen in on this conversation. "Revenge against whom?"

"My father."

"*Uh-huh*? And what did Daddy do to deserve your wrath?"

"He abandoned my mother and I, shortly after my conception."

"That's sad. Truly, I'm sorry for you. But I can't be of any assistance."

"Yes, you can, Lilly."

"How so, Froyd?"

"Let me put it this way," Froyd says. He uses his hands to frame his question. "If your husband was my father, that would make you my stepmother, and I your stepson. Is that right?"

Lilly's expression changes; her haughty demeanour falls. She nipped this idea in the bud with Vinnie in the restaurant, and now it's back again. Her instinct is to nip it again with Froyd, but something checks her. She's not angry; she is cautiously curious. If she were a cat, the hairs would be up on the back of her neck. There is so much mixed up in that idea; most, but not all of it, awful. She eyes Froyd intently while she processes the question. Damned it! He even looks like Tom Cata. Eventually, she says. "Don't be ridiculous."

"Is it really ridiculous to suggest that your husband mated with my mother twenty years ago?"

Lilly falls silent again. Her eyes fix on Froyd as the idea burrows through her mind, finding no resistance as it courses from one neuron to the next. It really does make sense, but she doesn't want it to.

Froyd interrupts. "Let's get the dates right. I am 24 years and four months old. A Millennial. Let's add nine months for gestation. Three minutes for the act. So, Lilly; what were you doing 25 years and one month ago when your husband was f**king my mother?"

Lilly answers in a monotone, "I was working my ass off setting up Chartreuse Capital."

"So, you were working your ass off, while your husband was shagging the ass off my mother. Did you know that?"

"You're blackmailing me," Lilly says, directly. "That's what this is about. This whole thing is a ruse. It's blackmail!"

"I told you I don't want your money. I want his. And I won't be around to spend it, remember. I'm dying shortly." Froyd is terse, impatient. "And I am not blackmailing you; I'm empowering you against your dick-head husband. Do you understand?"

From his trouser pocket, Froyd takes the memory stick and places it on the table. Then he removes the white envelope from his jacket. From inside, he retrieves folded documents and spreads them out on the table. He looks Lilly directly in the eyes, "Are you ready?"

Lilly nods her head, numbly. Hairs come up on the back of her arms, like the time in her car when Froyd first announced his plan for her. She feels vulnerable, like she has been playing with a Chess master and was about to get put into an embarrassing checkmate that exploited a foolish mistake she had made right at the beginning. Like inviting him into her car, for example.

Froyd points to the memory stick. "This contains

an audio file of my mother discussing my father. I got this a few months ago, before she passed. She names him, says how they met, what they got up to. I got very close to my mother, at the end. It's very intimate. She wanted to get it off her chest, and I wanted to hear it. It's all there. The affair went on for about five weeks. They f**ked like rattlesnakes, for your information. Are you with me?"

Lilly nods numbly and watches as Froyd adjusts the documents so that each is exposed, face-up.

He says, "These are copies, signed by a J.P. The originals are with my lawyer. His details are written on this envelope." Froyd points to each document in turn, "This is my birth certificate with mother's name, but no father's name. This is the paternity test results that connecting my DNA with your husband's and my mother's. This is my mother's bank statement showing the transfer of hush money. This is the gag order that she signed. The gag order is invalid now she's dead, hence the audio file." Froyd sits back in his stool, observing Lilly digest the information.

Her face drains of colour as her eyes dart across each of the documents, taking in the relevant details. It's not possible to verify their legitimacy, but the pattern is well and truly established. "How much?" she asks, gravely.

"How much what?"

"How much hush money?"

"$5.65 million Australian dollars."

"Shit!" Lilly brings her hand to her mouth, shaking her head in disbelief. That number is familiar.

"We're all in this together, Lilly. Do you understand? Tom Cata screwed my mother, he screwed me, he screwed you, and he's screwing the planet with his fossil fuel investments. So how about you and I make a deal to screw him back?"

Lilly looks up, surprised. "How?"

"Simple. I leave you with the documentary evidence, you rip him up in court, and we go halves in the loot. If you don't want to be personally involved in Chrysalis Day, I understand that, just gift the money to the Vita Foundation and they'll take care of it."

Lilly lifts a page on the bank statement to see that one line has been marked with a highlighter. She looks at the date, and the amount, shaking her head, astonished. "He said that money was for a Russian oil deal. It was one of our first trades. He said it went bad straight away. A learning experience, he called it. I just believed him. And here it really is."

"That paid for my tertiary education," Froyd says, chuckling. "Sorry for not graduating."

Lilly adjusts a seat and sits down. She inhales, and then breathes out through pursed lips.

"Just wait until you have a look at this," Froyd slides the manila envelope across the table.

Lilly intercepts it, and moves it aside, out of his reach. Instead, she says, "So, this explains why you took off in his helicopter that morning."

"Yeah. I wanted say 'hi' to daddy before I killed myself."

"And what happened?"

"He flew me to the airport. Gave me some cash and wished me well. That was nice of him. He didn't have to do that. I took a taxi home and got some groceries on the way."

"Did you explain how you came to be in the house?"

"I told him that I came looking for him, that you'd found me in the rain and took me in for the night. That's all."

Lilly nods, gravely. She inhales deeply, looking at the documents on the table. "Is there anything else?"

"No. That's all now."

"Good. I'll show you out."

At the door, Froyd holds out his hand and Lilly looks at it suspiciously. It seems a very formal gesture.

"Tomorrow's my flux day. I may not see you again."

"Oh, that's right. You are going to commit suicide," she says, sarcastically.

"That's scheduled for after midnight, but I am having a living wake from 6pm if you'd care to come along."

"I'll be busy then."

"Okay, then, Lilly. I hope you'll do the right thing."

"I always do the right thing, Froyd. Good night."

Lilly closes the door and watches as Froyd walks across the garden and exit through the gate. Then she goes back to the kitchen and sits at the table, staring at the documents.

After a while, she takes them to the lounge, sits in her chair, pours a drink, and then studies each one in fine detail. When she is convinced that they are genuine, she sends a text to Vinnie: "Hi Vin. Question. What was the name of the lawyer you used on your last husband?"

Divorce of the Century

In the morning, Lilly stands in front of the key rack in the garage choosing a car. Taking either the Bentley or the Mercedes is likely to lead to trouble, she thinks. There is something about being in a bad mood and driving a big, black car that makes her want to run people over.

While she's not dressed for the Jellybean, she takes it anyway, and drives to the restaurant on the jetty. She arrives ahead of time and sits at the table, motionless, in a sombre mood. The white envelope full of documents that Froyd left behind, rests on the table in front of her.

Vinnie arrives, all frivolous and light, but she quickly picks up on Lilly's mood, and adopts a suitably dour tone. "I was so excited when I got your text last night," she says. "The Lords are finally to split. This could be the divorce of the century."

Lilly nods pensively. "I learned a big lesson from the rose bushes, Vinnie."

"What was that?" Vinnie turns in her seat to look for a waiter. He is on the other side of the restaurant and seems to be ignoring her.

"Don't do things by half measures."

"How much do you think that he's worth?"

"Tom Cata has a fortune of around one hundred

and fifty million dollars."

"*Noice*. And how much do you think you'll get?"

"I won't stop until I get at least half."

"*Hooh!* He'll kick hard against that."

"He will be defenceless against what I have against him." Lilly taps a fingernail on the white envelope.

Vinnie is distracted and says, "You haven't ordered yet. I need a drink before I hear this." She twists in her seat to see the young male waiter. She raises her hand and clicks her fingers. This attracts his attention, but when he sees who it is, he turns and moves away, out of sight.

Vinnie turns back to Lilly. "He must have gone to get the drink list."

"You have to see this," Lilly says, gravely. She unfolds the paternity test document.

"What is this?"

"Documentary evidence that Froyd Denison is my stepson."

Vinnie's jaw drops open. She studies Lilly's face to confirm that she is serious. "*Shiiiit!* The dirty snake."

"Tomcat Lord has a bastard child, who happens to be an asshole. What is it with those genes?"

"Does that give you a claim on Froyd's house?"

Lilly shakes her head, "That's not the point."

"Oh, Christ, I need a drink." Vinnie turns in her seat and calls out, "Excuse me? Anybody?" She turns back to Lilly. "How can you be sitting there so calmly without even a Chardy?"

"So, the point is…" Lilly repeats.

"Yes. Yes. The point. What is the point?"

"I have documentary evidence that Tom fathered a child to another woman while he was married to me, and that he manipulated me to unwittingly pay her hush money out of Chartreuse Capital's trust account. That's a breach of Corporation's Act. You know what that means?"

"Jail time?"

"Leverage."

"*Shiiit,*" Vinnie sighs, stunned. "You can go for the lot."

Lilly nods her head. "I'll leave him his cars and his house, and maybe a few million for walking around money."

"What about the helicopter?"

"That will make a nice statue in the rose garden."

"Oh… my… God…" Vinnie sits back, stunned by the news.

"Now that, Vinnie, that is news." Lilly retrieves her phone and makes a call. She uses a sweet voice. "Oh, hello. My name is Lillian Lord. I am sitting at table 20. Could I please have a bottle of the

Semillon Blanc and two glasses? Thank you very much. Good bye."

Vinnie continues to stare aghast, processing the news, thinking about the black helicopter surrounded by rose bushes, with birds nesting under its rotor blades.

"So," says Lilly. "How are you today?"

The Flux Party

Later that day, Lilly is in the cocoon watching the TV when she hears the buzzer on the intercom. She moves to the CCTV display to see that someone is outside her front gate. It is a gaunt young man, wearing dreadlocks and a rainbow-coloured beany. He looks around furtively, as if he were being stalked. "Come on, come on," he says, impatiently.

"Who are you? What do you want?" Lilly demands.

"I'm Andy. Skinny's friend."

"Skinny?"

"Froyd Denison."

"What do you want?"

"He's having a party. He wants you to come."

"A party? What sort of a party?"

"What?" he asks, irritably.

"What sort of party is it?"

"What difference does it make? You're invited." Andy moves away from the intercom, out of sight.

Lilly returns to her chair and tries to put the conversation out of her mind. However, she is intrigued by the expression 'going to the flux'. She tries to ignore it but finds herself compelled to get to the bottom of it. She goes onto the Vita website and searches for the word. She finds that it describes the manner in which the elements that comprise a human's body returns to the soil or the air, depending on whether they are buried or cremated. Once back in the flux, other living things can absorb the minerals, to bring them back 'into life' again: revitalisation, this is called. It is a simple and compelling argument that reinforces the unbelievable idea that Froyd Denison plans to kill himself tonight.

"How might one celebrate one's last night?" Lilly wonders. Eventually, curiosity gets the better of her and she commits to going to the party. She takes the Bentley.

When she arrives at Roberts Road, she is surprised to see that it is cluttered with an assortment of vehicles raging from late model sedans to hippy vans, pushbikes and horses.

There is a kombi van parked next to the house and a cable running from it to the junction box on the wall. On the side, spray-painted in bright colours is the word: BioPowaVan. Next to this is a symbol that Lilly recognises, three overlapping circles surrounded by a two-thirds circle. The air is infused with the smell of popcorn as the biodiesel fuelled generator in the back of the van hums along, feeding electricity into the house.

The house is illuminated, and filled with dozens of joyous people, drinking, talking, or dancing to music. Froyd's party is in full swing.

Lilly parks the Bentley and walks into the crowd in the hallway. She hears someone call her name.

"Lilly!" Rae squeezes through the crowd and wraps her in a big hug. "I am so glad you came."

"Rae. What a surprise. What are you doing here?"

"It's Froyd's flux party. I'm not going to miss that."

Lilly then sees something that captures her immediate interest. On the inside of the right forearm, Rae is wearing a tattoo, the same shape as on the side of the van, logo of the Vita People.

Then a tall man wearing a rabbit skin waistcoat and daggy blue jeans squeezes past. The aroma of patchouli oil accompanies him, and Lilly is at taken aback by his presence. She browses him for a while, taking in all the detail. He wears a ponytail that rests on the top of his head, revealing a shaven nape where there is the Vita logo, tattooed.

Hairs creep up on Lilly's arms, as she finds herself uncertain of what it all means. One thing is for sure; she's surrounded by Vita People!

She looks back to Rae, and suspects that she has been watching her study the tall ponytailed man.

Rae makes a knowing snort and shakes her head. "We need to keep you on a leash."

"What?"

"This way." Rae ushers Lilly into the lounge where there is more breathing room. All the science papers have been piled up in the corner. There is more furniture than before, and a dozen people lounge around, chatting.

"So Froyd is going to kill himself tonight?" Lilly says, matter-of-factly.

"Yeah. He doesn't want to suffer, and he has completed the missions that he set himself." Rae says.

"But that's just wrong."

"It's right for him, Lilly. It's his life."

Just then, there is a cheer from the hallway, and a chanting and a commotion. The people in the doorway move aside and Froyd Denison enters the lounge room accompanied by two women. One is dressed in the uniform of a paramedic. He has his arm around a petite brunette scantily clad in lingerie and a cut down nurse uniform. Froyd looks exhausted, and elated at the same time. "Wow!" he says, "That was some medicine!" He kisses the girl on the forehead and then raises his left arm to show off the device that is attached to his wrist. The cannula hypodermic needle is pressed into his skin, held in place by tape. It is professionally done, obviously the work of the paramedic and not the hooker. Attached to the cannula is a small plastic tap.

Lilly stares at the device, gobsmacked, and her face turns ashen. She looks to Rae, anxiously, "What's going on?"

"He's all kitted up, look."

"What's the thing on his arm?"

"That's a cannula."

"I know that but why does he have a cannula?"

"That's his chosen method."

Lilly turns back to Froyd. Now he is moving to each of the people in the room, shaking their hand and pressing his forehead together with theirs, and saying the word, "Lagom."

"Lagom?" asks Lilly.

"It's a Scandinavian word. It means 'enough'."

"Enough? Enough of what?"

"Enough of anything, I guess. It's the appropriate amount. In this case, he is saying that he has lived enough. If he lives any more, he will have lived too much."

"What is this, some sort of suicide cult?" Lilly shivers, feeling a chill run through her body.

"Oh, Lilly," Rae says, disapprovingly. "It's Vita Belief." She shows off the logo on her arm.

"What? Are you all into it, here?"

"Most of us, I guess, to varying degrees. It's just a belief that nature is sacred and that we humans deserve to be happy. It's hardly controversial."

"And what about him?" Lilly indicates towards a man standing on his own, holding a glass of cola, and wearing a clerical collar.

"He's a priest, and an Vitan, too. It's a non-exclusive belief, you see. It doesn't clash."

"You have the tattoo on your arm."

"Yeah. I was one of the early adopters," Lilly raises her arm to show off the tattoo.

"Did Froyd invent Vita?"

"No, Froyd just runs the local chapter. It's all over the place now."

"And is killing yourself part of the belief?" Lilly asks.

"Killing yourself is not part of the belief, Lilly," Rae says firmly. "But making your own decisions about your life, is. And Froyd has decided to go back into the flux in a time and manner of his choosing. I'd never do that. I wouldn't be brave enough."

Froyd completes his Lagom dialogue with a man close by, and next moves over to Rae. He places his hand on her nape and presses his forehead against hers. "Lagom, Rae."

"Lagom, to you too, Froyd."

Froyd pushes his mouth onto Rae's mouth, and they kiss. Lilly squirms, unsure where to look.

Then Froyd turns his attention to Lilly. His face

lights up in a beaming smile, and he wraps an arm around her shoulder, the arm with the cannula protruding from it. Lilly glances at her shoulder, uncomfortable to have the medical device so close to her body. Froyd raises his right hand to draw attention, and says aloud, "This is Lilly Lord. She is my friend. Everyone say lagom to Lilly."

A roomful of Vita People follows the request, and there is a resounding, "Lagom, Lilly," almost as though it had been rehearsed.

Lilly blushes, but can't help the smile that crosses her face. She pats Froyd on the chest, saying, "Yes, and Froyd is my friend too. In a funny sort of antagonistic way."

"I want you to look after Lilly when I am gone. Okay?" Froyd tells his audience.

He turns to face her. "Thanks for coming, Lilly. I really appreciate it. Lagom. He places a kiss on her cheek, and then moves onto the next person.

"Lagom, Froyd." Lilly feels a chill run through her body, like when she sat in the car next to him. He seems so absolutely sure of himself. She finds herself in a daze watching the way people react to him. No one is trying to talk him out of his crazy suicide plan. She turns back to Rae and asks, "How do you know Froyd?"

"Oh, Froyd and I had a little fling years ago."

"A fling?"

"Yeah. He was going through this horrible corporate phase. He was on the verge of getting high distinctions in a finance degree. I swerved him away from that."

"It was you?" says Lilly, aghast.

"So, I was a cause in the Froyd Denison that you see today. Which means that I was also a cause in him getting irradiated in Fukushima."

"How do you feel about that?"

"Proud to have helped create a leader. Sad that he's subsequently dying."

"This is extraordinary," Lilly thinks. "These people have no fear of the truth."

The tall man with the Vita tattoo moves past again and Rae addresses him, "Skun Rabbit!"

"Oh, hi Rae," his voice is as soft as the pelt of his rabbit skin waistcoat.

"Skun, I'd like to introduce you to my sister, Lilly. Lilly, this is Skun Rabbit. He's a rabbit trapper. Amongst other things."

Lilly looks up into the man's warm, friendly eyes. She becomes light-headed as the patchouli oil washes over her. Skun Rabbit extends his hand, and Lilly instinctively does likewise. As soon as they touch, Lilly feels like she has herself become a rabbit, trapped in one of his snares.

In the Creek

When the party breaks, Lilly returns home, alone. She is in an ebullient mood as she sweeps through her house, turning on lights and activating the stereo system so that music bellows throughout the mansion. She retrieves the Brazilian wine that her *soon to be dragged through divorce courts husband* had delivered in his black helicopter. With a glass in her hand, she dances alone in the kitchen; and she has never done that before.

Then she goes to her cocoon, and searches the Vita website, following up on ideas that she had learned from the passionate and excited conversations with avowed Vitans. The buzz of the most extraordinary night of her life continues until two am when she finally shuts down the music and goes to bed. Half an hour later, she wakes and sits up, an uneasy feeling hugging her. She stares at the wall in a trance, a single idea looping over and over in her mind. Over the past few weeks, her empty life has become extremely full; full of new ideas, and even the hint of a purpose greater than gossiping with Vinnie and tormenting gardeners over their footwear. However, the person who is responsible – Froyd Denison – is on the verge of doing something incredibly stupid, if he hasn't already done it already.

"What would a Vita Person do in this situation?"

Lilly asks out loud. She ponders this question, conscious of the fact that she is not, herself, a Vita Person. "Action. It's all about being in action."

Lilly steps out of the bed, dresses, and goes to the garage. She glances up at the key rack, making the routine decision about which car to take. It occurs to her that she doesn't own a motor vehicle that would score a positive result on the Planetary Boundaries checklist. She shakes her head. There is no getting around that tonight.

She takes the Jellybean, and pulls up in front of Froyd's house. Everyone has gone, and the house is in darkness apart from the solitary LED light in the lounge room. She approaches the front door, sees an envelope pinned to the wood with the handwritten word 'John' on the front. She enters the building, calling his name but he's not there.

She takes the envelope off the door and sees that the flap is tucked into the back, not glued down, so she retrieves the contents. On one side of the sheet is a note explaining that his body can be found in a waterhole in the creek. On the reverse side, is a hand drawn mud map that shows a path through the forest, with an 'X' marking the spot. There is also a $50 bill in there, a tip for the undertaker, sort of.

Lilly returns to her car and retrieves a torch. Then, with the map in hand, she walks into the forest. It is very dark, a New Moon, and she is uncomfortable, never having forayed into the forest, despite living around it for decades.

It occurs to her that Vita People would likely feel comfortable in natural places, such as this, where she is only comfortable around human constructed environments that are sufficiently opulent. The sound of something moving in the undergrowth causes her to halt, training the torch beam in that direction. A shiver passes through her and she takes a few moments to compose herself. She checks the mud map, and then continues along the track.

When she arrives at the place that represents the 'X' on the map, she turns off the torch and searches around in the gloom, hoping to pick up faint noises. Close by, there is the sound of running water and a light, burning faintly.

She moves towards the light and sees Froyd, resting in a waterhole illuminated by a lamp. He is calmly humming a tune. He pours some wine into his glass, and Lilly can see that he still has the cannula in his arm. He clearly hasn't opened the tap yet, and he seems well at home in his waterhole, with the creek rushing around him in eddies.

Lilly's immediate thought is that it is highly unlikely that he would actually open the tap and kill himself. She thinks this despite Froyd having told her of his plan, despite her having found the note, and despite looking at him sitting there with the cannula sticking out of his arm. Despite all this, it still doesn't make sense.

Then Froyd raises his glass, as if to toast the forest. He says aloud, "I say farewell to all you who are extant. I have had lagom of being intact, and now choose to return to the biochemical flux from where I came. May my elements soon be revitalized in living tissue."

Froyd takes a swig of his wine, places his glass on a rock, and moves his right hand to the tap on the cannula. The creek water suddenly pulses red as Froyd's arterial blood courses through the metal tube.

Lilly is stunned. No sooner had she concluded that Froyd would not open the tap, and then he opens the damned tap! The sight of the blood in the water causes an immediate reaction. Lilly rushes forwards, stumbling into the creek. She lifts his hand and turns off the tap.

"What the f**k!" Froyd yells, angrily, pulling his arm away from her and fending her off with a foot. "What the f**ck are you doing!"

"You can't do that!"

"Who the f**ck are you to tell me that!" Froyd cradles his arm, grimacing.

"It's not your choice when to die," Lilly protests.

"It was not my choice to be born, you stupid bitch!"

She steps back awkwardly, up to her thighs in the creek. The rocks beneath her feet shift under her weight and she struggles to keep her balance.

Froyd settles himself back in his place, shaking his head angrily, "Keep the f**k away from me, woman. You are not invited to this." He grimaces as he places his hand over the cannula. "*Ahhh*. F**k! Now I'm in pain. Don't you ever think?"

"Okay, okay." Lilly steps up onto the riverbank, and rests on her haunches, her heart pounding. "I just don't think that you have the right to do this."

"Well, I don't think that you have the right to kill the f**king biosphere, baby-boomer."

"I want to help you."

"I won't be here." Froyd inspects the cannula in the light, checking to see that it is still in place.

"I mean, I want to help in general," Lilly says.

"Just open the damned envelope. It's not hard."

Lilly nods morosely. It's come back to the envelope again.

"Do you mind? I am on a clock now, Lilly. The medics will be coming for me soon. They face jail time if they get here and I am still alive. Do you want that?"

"No. I don't."

Froyd rests back in his waterhole, eyeing Lilly mistrustfully. The exertion has exhausted him, and he inhales deeply, a rasping noise coming from his throat. Lilly is reminded of his coughing fit in his house that rainy day. It looks as though he has been drained of the last of his energy.

"Do you want me to go?" she asks quietly.

Froyd rests his fingers on the tap on the cannula. He looks up at her, thinking it through. Then he shakes his head slowly. "Actually, there was something I overlooked."

"What's that?"

"To have someone here with me."

"Can I be that person?"

Froyd nods his head wearily, and Lilly shuffles forward, closer to him.

He says to her, "When it is over, you need to get that map back onto the door and disappear, you understand?"

"Yes. But what will…" Lilly is unable to complete her question, unsure whether it is appropriate to ask about these things.

"Just ask," Froyd says.

"What will happen to your body?"

"It will return to life soon."

A shiver rushes through Lilly's spine and exits the top of her head. She had not expected that reply. "Really? What does that mean?"

"Talk to Rae. She is organising it. I have to go now, Lilly," Froyd pleads.

"I understand."

Froyd opens the tap on the cannula, and then raises his hand and reaches out for Lilly. She moves closer and takes his hand between both of hers.

Blood pours from Froyd's body into the moving water. He makes a quiet gasp, as though he were feeling a sensation he had never felt before, or that he had been released from a pressing pain. For the best part of a minute, he rests silently, then his eyes roll back and fall closed.

Lilly watches, gripped by a morbid fascination. She is astounded at how much blood there is, pulsing in a billowing cloud, into the clear stream.

Froyd inhales sharply, and his eyes flicker open and fix on her. He licks his lips and says two final words. "Lagom, Lilly."

Then he closes his eyes, his body slumps, and he becomes motionless. After a few more moments, the blood stops flowing into the creek and the water runs clear around him.

Lilly feels Froyd's hand become limp and it slips from her grasp. It is almost as if it had defied gravity while he was alive, and now, upon his death, it was compelled by a natural force to move towards the ground.

She regains her grip, and then sits there holding his hand, conscious of the silence. She feels gooseflesh cover her body and the hairs on her arms seem to tingle with electricity.

The silence gives way to the sounds of the forest; the cicadas; the rustling of leaves in the breeze; the soft white noise of running water. She lowers his hand onto his chest, then steps back and looks at him from this new angle.

Froyd seems peaceful, like he were sleeping. This is how it ought to be, when one returns to the flux from whence they came.

Lilly steps back, her fingertips resting lightly on her lips. She thinks of the medics arriving at the house and having no map to guide them to the water hole. She backs away from Froyd Denison's body, and returns to redbrick house.

Reanimation Request

When Lilly wakes the next morning, she lies in bed forlornly staring at the ceiling. She is exhausted, emotionally drained, and feeling as though a big hole has opened up inside her. All the ebullience and excitement from the party has ebbed, leaving her stunned at the memory of having witnessed a man passing away. She rubs her palms together anxiously as she remembers the feeling of Froyd's hand in hers, slipping away as he died. She recalls the rollercoaster of emotions ranging from awe, respect, anxiety, sadness and anger.

Over breakfast, her mood changes as she sees Froyd's passing as just one incident in a whole chain of extraordinary events, and one that he had flagged to her, right from their first meeting in her car in the rain. A thought occurs to her, "What will the Vitans do with his body?" He had told her that he would be coming back to life and that Rae was looking after the details.

As Lilly ponders these things, her phone rings and she sees that Rae is calling. Her sister is in the area and asks if she can drop round.

Twenty minutes later, Lilly is laying out milk and cream for her younger sister, conscious of the fact that Rae doesn't know that she was with Froyd in his last minutes. She is in two minds about whether she should disclose that information. "What would a Vitan do?" she wonders. Unfortunately, no plausible answer presents itself, so she decides to hold onto her secret.

"I am glad that you are here," Lilly says, as she pours black coffee into the Jumbo Spode. "What are you planning to do with Froyd's body?"

Rae chuckles as if she had been asked an impossible question. "I am still trying to figure that out, actually."

"Really," Lilly asks, surprised. "I thought that you would have a ritual."

"Vita Belief is very young, Lilly. We are still working out these sorts of details. As it stands, the ritual is to honour the wishes of the deceased. But Froyd being Froyd, that's not so easy."

"I don't understand."

Rae retrieves a document from her bag and slides it across the table. "One of Froyd's emissaries delivered this to me, this morning."

Lilly opens the document, intrigued. It is a letter addressed to Rae, written on Vita letterhead and titled: Revitalisation Preference. Like all official Vitan written communication it opens with the word 'Lagom' and closes with 'oOo'. Lilly reads it through once, and then another time. Then she lays the document on the table, and looks at her sister, perplexed, "He wants to come back as a sea lion?"

"That's what it says."

"What does that even mean?"

"It means that he wants the minerals in his body reanimated inside a sea lion," Rae says, shaking her head, wearily.

"Well, how would you do that?"

"I am still trying to figure that out. The logical pathway is to get his minerals into some fish, then feed the fish to the sea lion."

"And how might you do that?"

"Again, I am making this up as I go along here. But this might work. When the body comes back from the hospital minus the donated organs, we could bury him in an Infinity Suit."

"I don't know what that is?"

"It's a garment that has been impregnated with micro-organisms that help speed up the decomposition process. His body will return to the flux quicker that way."

"Into the flux?"

"Into the soil in this case. Then we'll use the soil to grow some edible plants, alfalfa maybe, something that mullet can eat. We'll grow the mullet, then feed the mullet to the sea lion."

Lilly sits back in her seat, taken aback by it all. She wears a troubled and confused look.

"Now, if he had wanted to be reanimated in a

tree, like the Vitan People in Victoria, it would be so much easier; just bury him and plant a tree on top. But that's Froyd Denison, for you, I guess."

"Well, good luck with that," Lilly says. She slides the document across the table, washing her hands of the task.

"Now, I have a question for you," Rae says. "Have you taken a look at the Chrysalis Day proposal, yet?"

"Not yet I haven't, no," Lilly says, nonchalantly.

"Do you have an idea when you might do that?" Rae asks, cautiously.

"I don't have a plan for that, actually," Lilly says. She looks at Rae, conscious that her sister is not satisfied with her answer.

There is a pause while Rae considers her next words. "I'm pretty keen that you'd look into it because, Kara and I feature prominently in the plan, so I am told."

"*Uh-huh?*" Lilly says.

"So…"

"So?"

"So, maybe you could open it, please?"

"How about this?" Lilly says. "When I get around to it, I'll let you know."

"Well, I just hope that nothing goes extinct in the meantime," Rae says, flippantly.

"What does that mean?"

"It means that Chrysalis Day is a plan for transition, Lilly. It's a plan to help rapidly wean our planet off fossil fuels before we all get swallowed-up in a climate change catastrophe."

"That all sounds rather dark."

"Don't be glib," Rae says with an uncharacteristic tone.

"I am not being glib."

"It's serious business, Lilly. Treat Vita with gravitas, that's one of core principles."

Lilly senses edginess in Rae that she has never seen before. It reminds her of herself when she is in business mode, batting people aside with just the tone of her voice. For the first time, Rae comes across as a potential adversary, and Lilly doesn't know how to respond to that except to say in a non-confrontational voice, "Well, I am not a Vitan, so I am not bound by your rules."

"Vitans aren't bound by the rules either, Lilly. They chose to live by them because it fosters a better lifestyle for people and the planet."

"I see."

"And taking sustainability seriously is fundamental to anyone who wants to change the outcome."

"Well, I guess that I am just not there yet."

Rae collects her bag, and stands, shaking her head. "I don't know what the hell Froyd was thinking by making you the gate-keeper of Chrysalis Day," she says, frustrated.

"I didn't ask for it," says Lilly.

Rae moves towards the door and turns to look at her elder sister. "I still love you Big Sis. But you really need to grow up," she taps her hand over her heart, suggesting that the growth is emotional. Or spiritual.

Lilly Morose

Days later, Lilly sits at the kitchen table with a Jumbo Spode cup full of coffee. She is staring at the white tiles, mesmerised. She shakes her head, coming out of the trance, exhausted to have the events of the past few weeks rattling around inside her head. Lilly Lord, the gatekeeper of Chrysalis Day; the idea horrifies her. She doesn't want to be the gatekeeper of anything, except helicopters and white wine, maybe.

She begins to wish that she had never heard of Froyd Denison. Why had he chosen to inflict his attentions on her, and not some other wealthy Duffys Forest boomer woman? There was plenty of those to choose from and some much richer than her. And this idea that Froyd is actually Tom Cata's lovechild. The idea is too horrendous to contemplate, so she puts it out of her mind.

In its place, another thought. In the weeks that Froyd had been in her life, she had discovered new and exciting ways of living, new things to think about. He had helped to bring her out of the torpor that she had been in ever since Tom took over running Chartreuse Capital, and she was able to withdraw to her introversion and solitude. How long had she been like that? 10 years? 20 years? What had she done in that time? That was half of her adult life; where did it go?

Lilly sighs, feeling a shudder run through her. She doesn't like thinking about that, and yet it is the only thought that she has. To numb it, she goes into her wine cellar and spends an afternoon perusing, finally emerging with a crate containing a selection of wines that match the diverse strands of her mood.

She withdraws for days into her cocoon with the drapes closed so that she doesn't even get to see the gardeners tending the helicopter-denying rose bushes. She goes online and spends hours browsing clothing, watches, holidays, and new colour options for house and the Jellybean.

During this period, she takes a call from her sister, Rae. She opens up to Rae, telling her that Froyd's passing has greatly shaken her and she thinks that it was fundamentally wrong. Rae says that she feels the opposite; that Froyd having taken control of his own destiny encourages her.

"But he was your friend," Lilly says.

"Yes. And he lived his life how he wanted. How 'he' wanted."

"But he didn't have to kill himself."

"That's right. He didn't have to kill himself. He could have chosen to suffer a slow, painful death. He was free, and he didn't 'have' to do anything, so he chose what to do."

"I guess," Lilly sighs, exhausted from trying to

convince Rae to share her view.

"So have you found out what his plan was?" Rae asks.

"I haven't looked yet. It's all too overwhelming."

"You should check it out. I'm dying to know."

"How come you don't know about it?"

"He said that you would brief me."

"Okay, I'll take a look. I'll call you back sometime."

After the call with Rae, Lilly retrieves the manila folder and tosses it onto the seat opposite. The corner of the flap is lifted, reminding her that she had got at least part way to opening it one time before.

She sits in her chair looking at the envelope feeling a mixture of curiosity, frustration and anger towards it. How audacious that someone would make a plan for her life, and how badly she needs a plan for her life.

Eventually, she picks up the courage to look at the contents of the file and she leans forward to retrieve it. At that moment, she is alerted to a familiar noise. The sound of a gas turbine engine and the beating of rotor blades; Tom Cat is back!

Lilly moves to the windows and pulls the drapes aside and watches the chopper touch down, just beyond the rose bushes. What's worse, she sees the downdraft tear the leaves and petals from the few flowers that have bloomed. They fly through the air in eddies of fast wind, and pelt against the bay windows a few inches from her nose.

Lilly shakes her head angrily. She retrieves her phone and calls her head gardener. The call goes to message bank and she says tersely, "Rudy, this is Lillian Lord. I want to see a plan for extending the rose bushes all the way down the back wall. Call me back, please."

She watches Tom walking up the garden with his brief case and a bottle of wine. She feels the anger rise inside her when she remembers that she had started the process of divorcing the philandering old cat but got distracted by Froyd's suicide. Then she feels vulnerable because she is wearing her dressing gown, without make-up, and her cocoon is a mess.

Tom enters the house, calling out for her, "Where's my little kitty cat?" He finds her standing in the bay windows, dithering.

Tom looks around the cocoon, at the signs of *binge melancholia,* the disarray, empty wine bottles, snack food containers. He chuckles. "Well, you've been busy."

"I have been dealing with emotionally sensitive issues and I would appreciate your empathy." Lilly adjusts her dressing gown and returns to her seat.

"Well, I am all empathy, today, Lilly." Tom lowers himself onto the chair opposite, sitting on the manila envelope. He opens his briefcase, retrieves a sheaf of documents, and places them on his lap. He has an exuberant demeanour that he uses when he has an exciting business proposal to share.

Lilly observes him observing her, waiting for an imprimatur to begin. Instead, she eyes him suspiciously, thinking that she wouldn't be sitting here, feeling miserable if he hadn't shagged Froyd's mother all those years ago. Should she tell him that she knows? Should she tell him that she is going to divorce him and plunder his treasure? "Keep your powder dry," she thinks. There will be a right time to drive that spear into him. She nods her consent for Tom to begin.

"So, as you know, there is the annual general meeting of the shareholders at Chartreuse Capital and I need you be in action to get this proposal approved by the majority, that's five of the nine directors."

Lilly nods, recognising two things, that Tom is onto something big, and that he is the second person to offer a plan for her life. "Like father, like son," she thinks.

Tom continues, "Then, once the agreement has passed, I want you to operationalize this plan. You will be full time on this for six to eight weeks. Then you can sit back and smell the…" Tom dithers, for a second. Finally, he is able to complete his sentence. "Smell the champagne bubbles."

After the briefing, Lilly stands in the bay windows watching him depart. The downdraft from the chopper strips the rose bushes of the last of their buds. Once the noise of the chopper has receded, she looks back to the chair opposite where there are now two documents dictating how she ought to live her life.

Tom's document is the more familiar of the two, so she opens this and browses through the contents. It's an operational plan for Chartreuse Capital to undertake a capital-raise to fund the establishment of a US coal seam gas company in rural Australia. She browses the financial projections and sees that the hedge fund stands to make a considerable return. As she browses the documents, she keeps seeing the word 'fracking' and at every instance, she thinks of Froyd, and her eyes drift to the manila envelope. It is still on the chair, now crumpled and squashed from the weight of Tom's ass.

She feels both remorseful about Froyd's passing, and pressured that his dying wish was for her to follow his instruction. And she feels angry that she should be feeling this way.

She glances back to Tom's documentation, the

financial projections, and she feels like she is on familiar territory. She retrieves her phone, moves to the bay windows, and calls Tom. He is still in flight and the call is punctuated by the sound of the helicopter, so she keeps it brief.

"Are these numbers right?"

"Oh, they're right, alright."

Lilly hangs up and stands with the Chartreuse Capital document in her hand. She looks down at the squashed manila envelope on the chair – the Chrysalis Day proposal. Curious, she picks it up and holds it in her other hand and weighs them both. Tom's document has the familiar feel to it. She knows that it will be stuffed with spreadsheets and contracts and financial projections. This is all familiar territory for Lilly, and it could be welcome distraction from her torrid thoughts about Froyd and his annoying Chrysalis Day plan.

Then her phone starts ringing. Lilly tucks the documents under her arm and retrieves the phone from her pocket. Vinnie is calling, and it has been days since she has spoken to her friend.

Lilly moves to a sideboard and slides open a drawer. She shoves Froyd's manila folder inside and then closes the drawer.

She takes the call, holding Tom's shale proposal in front of her. "Hi, Vinnie," she says, excitedly. "Have I got news for you?"

Bristlebird Nest

Two months later…

Lilly pulls the Bentley to a halt outside the front wall of her Duffys Forest mansion, and fumbles around in her handbag for her smartphone. She activates the app that opens the gate and, as it rolls open, she observes the state of the hedge in front of the wall. It most certainly does not look like the hedge pictured in the brochure of the house twenty years ago. The growth has thrown stems up into the air in all directions. It no longer looks as though someone of means cares it for, and that will not do.

"Note to self," Lilly says, "Get the damned hedge fixed."

Inside the house, there is a mountain of mail on the kitchen table, dutifully piled by the house servant. There are numerous official white documents and plastic-wrapped mining and finance journals. Lilly flicks through, looking for something out of the ordinary. She finds correspondence from a law firm that she initially doesn't recognise. Then she remembers; it's from that special project called: *sue Tom Cata*. She hasn't thought of that project for weeks. Nonetheless, she opens the envelope to find a letter confirming that all of Froyd Denison's legal documents check out as authentic.

Lilly sighs. She has no interest in battling Tom, right now. In fact, she's feeling quite charitable towards Tom Cata, right now.

She pulls open the fridge and retrieves a bottle of the *Cuvee Guesse*, pops the cork, and pours a healthy glass. Then she departs for the backyard, glass in hand.

In her absence and on her instruction, the gardener has extended the helicopter denying rose bushes all the way to the back wall. One hundred and thirty metres of bristling prickles shimmer in the sunlight like the sharpened tips of spears of an eager army. Lilly walks the length of the yard, watching the manner in which the light plays along the rows. She is reminded of driving in the French countryside, in her younger years, watching the same trick of light playing-out in the rows of grave vines. That was with Tom, when they were courting, in the days before Chartreuse Capital.

Lilly reaches the far wall and turns to look back at her mansion. Something about the colour of the walls ticks her off and she makes a note to check out some new colour schemes. Also, these rose bushes aren't really doing it for her anymore. She is bigger than Tom Cata and his stupid helicopter. She won't have him interfering with her peace of mind any longer. She is, after-all, Lillian Lord, and she has just left her mansion in the forest to play in corporate Australia, and she kicked ass.

Back in the kitchen, she refills her glass and calls her gardener. His wife answers, apologising profusely, saying that he has been unable to attend work due to an injury.

"What sort of injury?" Lilly asks, curious what kind of wound could disable the man who planted the sea of thorns.

"He got pricked by a rose thorn," the wife says. "The wound got infected and he's been bed-ridden for a week."

"Well, that does it," Lilly thinks, looking out at the offending bushes. "The roses have to go."

"Could you ask your husband if he could recommend a replacement?" Lilly enquires. Minutes later, the wife returns to the line and passes the number of a person who just goes by the name Big Alan.

The following morning, Big Alan the gardener arrives. Despite his name, he is not big. He is short, wearing op-shop clothes and a grin the size of a full-grown Cheshire Cat's. Lilly's first instinct is to ask what he is smiling at, but she resists the temptation. Instead, she walks with him to the front gate and quizzes him about his hourly rate, availability and the sorts of work that he his is comfortable to take on.

At the gate, she hands him a copy of the brochure

that she had been given by the estate agent, decades ago. She waves her hand at the offending hedge, "That ought to look like that."

"Piece of cake," says Alan, chirpily.

Lilly looks the short fellow over, uncertain whether he is the right guy for the job. She decides to persevere, and so escorts him to the shed where there is a dazzling array of gardening equipment. "So, I'll just leave it with you, I guess."

"Yes, Ma'am."

"If you need anything, I'll be inside. Just knock on the back door." Lilly regrets having said this the moment the words come out. She returns to the lounge room and tries hard to resist the temptation to spy on Alan as he walks from the shed to the front gate, carrying battery operated hedge trimmers. She has a sneaking suspicion that his socks won't meet her approval, but she doesn't want to be conflicted about sending him home when she needs the job done.

Shortly, Alan knocks on the back door and Lilly curses herself for having put the idea into his head, in the first place. She pulls open the door, expecting to be cranky, but Alan's demeanour prevents this. Instead, she is just officious. "Is there a problem?"

"No problem," Alan says, cheerfully. "Actually, something worthy of a celebration."

"You've finished the job ahead of time?" Lilly

quips.

"Haven't even started, actually."

"Why not?"

"There's a Bristlebird nest in the hedge. With an egg."

"What is that? Some sort of…" Lilly is perplexed as to why she is even having this conversation with the funny little man.

"It's a sort of bird, really," Alan says, thoughtfully.

"Can you just move the nest?"

"Oh, I can't do that," Alan chuckles, as if the proposal was right on the edge of daft. "We should just leave it until the chick flies off."

"How long will that be?"

"Oh, well now," Alan draws a deep breath as though he had been asked to answer the meaning of life. He cradles his chin in his fingers and shakes his head, thinking it through. "Could be four weeks. Maybe five."

"Four weeks? That hedge will have consumed the whole property by then. Can't you just move the nest?"

"Oh, no, Ma'am. That won't do."

"Well in that case, I guess I'll just have to get someone else to complete the job."

"That won't work, either Mrs Lord." Alan takes a

step back, unsure of his position.

"And why not?"

Alan dithers, then straightens up, "It would be illegal for you to authorise that nest be disturbed, now that you have been notified that it contains an endangered."

"Illegal? A what?"

"There's wildlife laws, you see."

"What? Are you going to report me?" Lillian asks, indignantly.

"I'm duty bound to protect the endangered," Alan says, humbly. "They are sacred."

"Duty bound? Sacred to whom?"

"I am duty bound to protect endangered species, Mrs Lord."

"What are you? David Attenborough?" Lilly scoffs.

"No, ma'am. I am Vitan."

"Rubbish," Lilly says spontaneously. Then she takes a breath, surprised at her own comment. There's that word again: Vitan. Barely a day has she been back in her home and there is a self-professed Vitan in her doorway. "Where's your tattoo, then?" she demands.

"I don't have a tattoo."

"I thought all Vitans had tattoos."

"I know this Vitan chick called Carly. Boy, she's

got that Vitan symbol tattooed all over her. All over, and all under. Do you know some Vitans, Mrs Lord?"

"I've met a few," Lilly concedes. She finds her resistance to the little man slip to a comfortable place, and decides to go easy on the endangered bird, as well. The pressing issue of the rose bushes comes to mind.

"Okay, let's leave the hedge for now. There's another job needs doing. And I doubt there'd be anything nesting in the roses."

Burn the Rose Bushes

Lilly steps outside with Alan and walks with him to the wall at the far end of the yard. Alan is amazed at the extraordinary sight, the serried ranks of thorns with not a shred of wildlife to be seen. He mumbles to himself, rubbing has palm over his head, "Why would you do this?"

"I want them all gone," Lilly says. "Just get them out of here as soon as possible. Can you handle that?"

"Might have to get a few extra hands."

"Whatever you need to do. You'll be paid."

"And a truck or a wood-chipper, maybe. What do you want put in their place?"

"What do you suggest?"

"I know some people looking for a site for a willow coppice." Alan chuckles, as if he has said something audacious.

"What is that?"

"It's a plantation of willow trees. They cut them every year and they grow back."

"Why would they do that?"

"For the wood. For a ceremonial fire, you see."

"And what's the ceremony?"

"Earth New Year."

Lilly chuckles. "You wouldn't want to be burning

things in January. It's the height of the fire season."

"No, no. This is Earth New Year. In July."

"What?" Lilly stops in her tracks. "Why is it that you Vitans have to make everything so complicated? There is a perfectly good New Year's already."

"I'm not so sure of that. You know what the first of January actually celebrates, don't you?" Alan asks.

Lilly doesn't, and she feels vulnerable in her ignorance. This is clearly Vitan wisdom, of which she knows herself to be sorely lacking. "It celebrates the beginning of the year," she says, as if repeating herself makes her ignorance less obvious.

"It's the feast of the foreskin," says Alan, plainly.

"I beg your pardon?"

"January first is an ancient celebration: the Feast of the Circumcision of Christ. It doesn't speak to sustainability and happiness at all. Earth New Year does, but."

Like the rabbit in the headlights, or the whale with the harpoon set firmly in its spine, Lilly finds herself hooked on Vita Belief again. She feels a craving for new knowledge, and a pang of conscience for being so prickly with the stranger. She turns her gaze on Alan and he catches her eye. It is an odd look and Alan glances at the ground, not knowing how to respond.

"Alan, how about I make you a cup of coffee and you tell me more about Earth New Year?"

"Don't you want me to get started on the roses?"

"Don't worry. You're still on the clock. Come and have a coffee with me."

Inside the kitchen, Lilly points to a stool next to the bench and instructs Alan to, "Sit."

She sets about preparing the coffee and okays the diminutive gardener to bring her up to speed.

"You understand the idea behind the New Year, I guess?"

"Why don't you tell me your version?" Lilly scoops coffee grounds into the pot and settles it on the stove.

"Well, a year is the time it takes our planet to make one complete circuit around the Sun. It's sort of like a circle, so it doesn't really have a start point or end point."

Lilly turns and crosses her arms. She holds her face in such a manner that Alan feels like he has an audience.

"So, the choice of what day you should call the end or the beginning of that annual cycle is arbitrary. And there are dozens of New Years days. Chinese, Persian, Indian, they all have different calendars. And the beginnings of the calendars all speak to some culturally relevant event."

As Alan speaks, Lilly finds herself enchanted by the iconoclastic audacity of Vita Belief. The rewriting of all that is taken for granted that doesn't serve the simple goals of sustainability and happiness. The honesty of it: calling black, black; white, white; and acknowledging the million shades of grey for what they really are: simply grey. She remembers her conversations with Froyd. Back then, she felt like she was being told the truth for the first time in her life. It was like talking to someone who is adult enough to not believe in Santa anymore. He used the term 'non-infantile' as though all other conversations by adults amounted to the maturity of babies.

Lilly aches. She wants to be involved in Vita. But not in the trenches like an Vitan Gardener, or the guy who kills himself in the creek. She wants to stand over it, wearing designer wellington boots. Involved, but at arms-length. No tattoos, no obligations; an occasional benefactor, maybe. A good ear, perhaps. Maybe she can host one of their parties.

She interrupts Alan, mid-sentence. "So, it's in July, you say. Earth New Year."

"On the 16th."

"Why the 16th?"

"It's beginning of the Anthropocene Epoch. Maybe."

Lilly is distracted by the noise of the pot, boiling. Alan stops talking and watches as she ceremoniously lays out the coffee: the pot, the Spode, saucers, milk, cream, spoons, biscuits and plates.

Finally, Alan has a cup, and Lilly rests back against the sink, holding her coffee close to her nose, inhaling the rich scent. She nods, giving the new gardener the imprimatur to continue his story.

He starts with a recap. "Vita is a new environmental philosophy that seeks to connect people to the natural world. So rather than having cultural ceremonies that are connected to human constructs like religious things or monarchs, we connect them to natural phenomena. So, we celebrate Full Moons. We celebrate equinox and solstice, extreme weather events, and biological phenomena, like the first sighting of a migratory species. We also celebrate the turning of the year. Earth New Year."

"Yes, yes, I am with you. But the sixteenth of July?"

"Well, that's the day that we started testing nuclear weapons. And that chemical signature is now visible all around the world in the soils and rock. Geologists like this because it helps to define the beginning of an epoch: the Anthropocene. This is the era in which humans are the main drivers of physical processes on this planet."

Lilly nods at length, taking it all in. The reasons behind it all are fascinating; but that's not what she wants to know. "What do you do on the sixteenth of July?" she asks, frostily.

"Oh, I see," Alan says, changing tack, "Well, we get lots of people together. Have a big fire, set off the Gadget to commemorate the Trinity Bomb test. Drink. Eat. Talk. Get merry, I guess. It's just a party, really."

"You have a big party?"

"Yes."

"Then why don't you have it here?" Lilly asks. "You won't have time to grow your willows, so burn the rose bushes, instead."

Alan glances out the kitchen window at the brown sea of thorns extending over one hundred meters to the far wall. He nods at length as he thinks it through.

"Can we plant the coppice here, after?"

"Let's just burn the rose bushes first, shall we?"

The CH Fund

Later in the day, Vinnie arrives to take Lilly out to lunch. Vinnie is brimming with excitement, having not seen nor heard of Lilly for weeks. Today, she is sporting a new vehicle, an Audi. It still has the little tendrils on the tyres, and that distinctive new-car smell, albeit masked with fragrance.

"And how are you?" Lilly asks, leaning across to kiss her girlfriend.

"Happy day," Vinnie says, cheerily. "New car day." She taps the steering wheel, a proxy of the whole vehicle. Once Lilly is buckled in, Vinnie drives out the gates, and speeds up along the road.

"Where are we going?" Lilly asks.

"Normal place. The Jetty."

"You be nice to the waiter now," Lilly jests.

"What does that mean?"

"Oh, you torment him terribly. Poor thing. He's only about twelve."

"Not so! Well… No less than he deserves."

They laugh together, and Lilly pats the back of Vinnie's hand that rests on the gearshift.

"It's so good to see you," she says, enthusiastically.

"What have you been doing? You just vaporised."

"I have been a slave for finance," Lilly sighs. "I've been putting together a capital raising document with Tom."

"*Ohhh.* Working with the Tom Cat. What's the project?"

"It's a convertible note."

"Really? A private offering or…?"

Lilly retrieves a brochure from her purse. She straightens it out, and then hands it over.

Vinnie scans it briefly as she drives. The logo shows a stylized wellhead and flame, and the name 'CH Fund'. "It doesn't have the Chartreuse branding."

"It's a new vehicle, owned by Chartreuse," Lilly tells her.

"Why did you do that?"

"Risk mitigation."

"What risk?"

"Fracking has a reputation risk profile that we didn't want to bring into the main fund which is just coal and conventional oil."

"*Hmmm.*" Vinnie murmurs. "What's the return?"

"Eight point four per cent, quarterly, over three years."

"Eight per cent. That's good for these days. Should I come in, do you think?"

"I can't advise you of that." Lilly says. "Talk to

your accountant." She chuckles and glances at her friend.

"You are so ethical," Vinnie says, laughing. "When's the placement?"

"In a few weeks. I get the contracts back from the lawyer, open the trust account, and then we are away."

"Well, there will be a lot of smiles going around then."

"You'll like this," says Lilly, changing tack. "Alan says that we need to dissociate being tall or handsome or well dressed or rich or well connected, from being happy." The words just flow out of Lilly's mouth as though they we completely normal things for her to say.

"Who?" asks Vinnie.

"Alan. He says that we don't need a reason to be happy. We just need to 'be' happy."

"I'm happy to hear it," says Vinnie, perplexed. "What is this? Some new app?"

"App? What?" Lilly asks.

"The Happy Alan App?"

"It's not an App. I am talking about Alan, my gardener."

"Oh, you have a gardener called Alan."

"Yes. He's a diminutive man, but very wise." Lilly ponders her statement for a while.

"He's not one of those Froyd types, is he?"

"He's an Vitan. They are very wise, the Vitans," Lilly concludes.

"I thought that you would have outgrown them. What with your recent activities, and all." Vinnie says.

"What does that mean?"

"Haven't you just been fraternising with frackers?"

"So?"

"Well, isn't that exactly the opposite of what Vitans would do?"

Lilly mumbles and turns her face towards the side window. Silently, she watches the houses and trees moving past.

Vinnie glances across, wondering how the light-hearted conversation had soured so quickly. "*Anyhoo…*" she says, letting her words hang in the air.

Lilly adjusts her sunglasses, feeling a strange sense of foreboding. A jumble of thoughts flashes through her mind. They complete with the memory of Vinnie sitting in her lounge room reading off a piece of crumpled paper the words, "Froyd fell in frack fluid."

"So, what have you tasked the philosophical garden gnome with doing?" Vinnie asks, grinning.

"He's ripping up the roses." Lilly lowers her sunglasses and looks directly at her friend. She is sombre, as she returns to the previous point of conversation. "It's a very good point, actually. Your point."

"What is?"

"The Vitans and the capital raise. They are mutually exclusive."

"*Pah!* I wouldn't worry about it?"

"No?"

"*Nahh*. Do you remember Sonya Minks?"

"Minks? The health food franchise?"

"Yeah."

"What about her?" Lilly asks.

"She's as fat as a house."

"So?"

"So... What you do at work and what you do at home needn't be the same thing. Chartreuse Capital, that's serious, adult business that you do during the paying hours. And Vita, that's your little plaything. As long as you don't mix them up, you'll be fine."

"Really?" Lilly slides her glasses back in place.

Vinnie pulls the car to a halt in the parking bay adjacent to the Church Point Restaurant. "Are you hungry?" she asks as she pulls the handbrake on.

"I'm thirsty," Lilly's smile returns. "And you're

driving."

New Year's Committee

When Lilly returns home she is tipsy. The discussion with Vinnie in the car has her feeling at ease to enjoy the Vitans as her after-hours activity. Vinnie, for all her faults, was very concise in her advice.

Off the hook, she looks into the yard, feeling a flash of excitement, like she was a child again. At short notice, Alan has rounded up three mates and they are all busy hauling rosebushes from the ground.

Lilly changes into colourful, designer outdoor clothes and dons a pair of wellingtons that have pictures hand-painted on the sides. She trudges down the yard holding a silver tray that contains a jug of lemon squash and four glasses, each filled with block ice. She calls out to the workers, and they gather around, enthusiastically accepting the cool break.

"How's it all coming along?" she asks as she fills the glasses from the jug.

"They're coming up really easily, actually," Alan says. "They root system is barely developed. How long have they been in there, do you think?"

"Oh, about four weeks," Lilly says, nonchalantly.

"Four weeks?" asks one of Alan's workmates, surprised. He's a stocky fellow, in his sixties, wearing a tatty old hat. "You know, in the Army, they use this sort of vegetation around the perimeter of military bases."

"Whatever for?" Lilly asks, disingenuously.

"Area denial. To keep the bad guys out."

"Not the sort of thing you'd expect in a country manor," quips one of the others.

"And that's why I am having you tear them out by the roots," Lilly says. "So, what's your plan, Alan?"

"We'll just keep pulling them up, I guess. Shake the mud off and pile them up in the corner over there."

"Pile them up in the middle, where the fire will be" Lilly says. "Then we'll lay turf all around for the party."

"I thought that the coppice was going in here," says the Army guy.

"I haven't decided on the coppice yet," Lilly says. "But I have decided on the party."

"The party?" asks Alan.

"We're having Earth New Year's here, aren't we?"

"I don't make that call, Mrs Lord. That's agreed by the committee."

"The committee? Right. Well how long is it going to take you to convince your committee?"

"Well, I don't know. They're hard-nosed bastards." Alan looks around at his mates, and they all break into laughter.

"So, this is your committee?" Lilly says, looking at each of the workers with newfound interest. "So, you are all Vitans?"

"To varying degrees," says the Army guy. "This bloke here can't make up his mind." He nods towards his companion, who just shrugs. "He's an honorary Vitan. And not on the committee."

"So, what do you say?" Lilly asks. "I have been working these past few months and I fancy some recreation. So, I'll pay for the catering, which will be fitting to the venue. The roses are your firewood. I guess you'll look after the invite list and whatever else you need to make it a night to remember."

Alan nods, thinking it through. He turns to his Army mate. "What do you reckon, Geoff?"

Geoff takes off his tatty old cap and holds it against his chest. "It's a very decent offer. Thank you, Miss."

"Mrs Lord. No. Call me Lilly."

"Thank you, Lilly. It's a very kind offer. I'm just not sure there's enough room."

"Enough room?" Lilly laughs, surprised. "The yard is the size of a football field. How many Vitans are there?"

"It's not the people that's the issue. It's the Gadget."

"Oh, yeah, the Gadget," Alan agrees. The others join in with a sinister chuckle.

"This must be a private joke," Lilly says.

"It's a pyrotechnic that we let off, on the night," Alan says. "Just a few flames,"

"Yeah, just a few flames," Geoff scoffs.

"Then we'll get the fire brigade on standby," Lilly says. "I donate to them, you see. I'm sure that they'll be happy to oblige."

"Well, I'm open to it. What do you guys reckon?" Alan asks his mates. The three men move into a huddle and confer on the matter. Lilly watches as they turn and face the house, wave their arms in the air, and debate various aspects of the plan. Eventually, they turn back to Lilly, nodding in unison.

"We've got to have the fire brigade on stand-by."

"I'll call them in the morning," Lilly says.

"Best I call them," Geoff says. "Technical reasons."

"Then I'll wait your call in the afternoon," Lilly holds the tray out. "Glasses?"

Lunch with Rae

News of the upcoming New Year's celebration spreads quickly in the Vitan community. Shortly, Lilly takes a call from Rae, her younger sister. They have not seen each other for months, since Rae told Lilly to 'grow up'. Feeling bold, Lilly invites Rae to lunch at Café Sydney, and Rae accepts.

Shortly, they are seated at the table in the restaurant that overlooks Circular Quay. They wait silently as the waiter pours chilled Chablis into their glasses. Lilly nods her thanks as the waiter departs.

"I don't know whether I was more surprised or excited to hear that you were hosting Earth New Year," Rae says. "I got you something." She lifts a heavy, wrapped package from her bag and places it on the table.

"I am hosting the party in honour of our mutual friend, Froyd," Lilly says. "What's this?"

"This is a little present from me to you," Rae awkwardly lifts the object from the table and hands it over.

"*Offf*. It's not so little." Lilly turns the object, looking for the logical place to tear the wrapping.

"It's re-useable wrapping," Rae frowns.

"Sorry. Is it customary to give gifts on your New Years?"

"No. That's just the aberration called Christmas," Rae chuckles. "The evil lovechild of capitalism and Christianity."

"Now, now. Don't be like that. Are you saying that Vitans don't celebrate Christmas?"

"Some do; families, mainly. But Vita has its own celebrations."

"Yes. Alan mentioned this. What were they?"

Rae counts them off on her fingers, "Full moons, equinoxes, solstices, extreme weather events, seasonal biological phenomena, and Earth New Year. Oh, and some new ones in the pipeline including Galactic Core Night and Cosmos 1818. That's a fashion parade."

"My goodness. What have you got yourself into?" Lilly says. The wrapping paper falls away revealing a coffee table book with a hard cover. The cover has a black background, and in the middle a bright, orange mushroom cloud rises out of a desert. Lilly reads the title, aloud, "*A Thousand Suns. A photographic history of nuclear weapons.*" She places the book on the table, unsure how to react. "Right."

"It's a passaround book. Once you're finished with it, pass it on," Rae says, humbly. "Very hard to get hold of."

"And it's very hard to lift. Is there a reason why you bought me a book on nuclear weapons?" Lilly asks.

"Of course. You are hosting the Earth New Year party. I think that it's important to know why we celebrate the things that we do. That way, we don't end up with a quarter of the world's population celebrating a foreskin, every year."

Rae flips to a well-thumbed page that shows a black and white photo of two men in a cabin in the desert. In the foreground is a bulky, technical object with cables hanging out of it. It's like something out of a 1950s science fiction movie; as well it might, as this is the physics package of the 'Gadget'.

"This is the Trinity test," Rae says. "I didn't choose the name, by the way. But this explosion is at the heart of Earth New Year."

The Gadget is the name affectionately given to the first-ever nuclear bomb to be exploded. It was a plutonium-implosion device, of the type destined to be dropped on the Japanese city of Nagasaki. It was much more complex weapon than the simple uranium device planned for Hiroshima, and the bomb technicians wanted to test the design before deploying it in combat. So, on 16 July 1945, in the New Mexico desert, the Gadget, set in a cabin atop a tower, was detonated. The bomb worked as planned, releasing energy equivalent to 17,000 tonnes of TNT high explosives. First, a bright flash in the desert – brighter than a thousand suns – then a terrible orange ball of flame, rising; the hot gas inside, roiling and angry; the outer edge of the fireball cooling and falling, giving it the distinctive mushroom cloud shape, like a mutant fungus growing into the sky.

Rea flicks to another page. Here is a bizarre image, showing what looks like a snowball has been dropped and squashed on the floor, against a black background. The upper half of the snowball is smooth and round, but the lower part is crumpled and spread out.

"This is the fireball a fraction of a second after detonation," Rae says. "The top of the fireball is 200 metres high."

"I don't understand why Vita would celebrate a nuclear bomb." Lilly says, now intrigued with the book. She flips through some pages as Rae responds.

"We're not celebrating the bomb, *per se*. We commemorate what the bomb signifies, the beginning of a new geological epoch in which humans are the main driving force of change on the planet. The Trinity Bomb Test is a de-facto date for the beginning of the Anthropocene Epoch, you see."

"Alan mentioned that. He didn't sound so sure, though."

"The Trinity bomb test is a proposed start date of

the Anthropocene. It hasn't been officially decided yet."

"By whom?"

"The geologists," Rae waves her hand, dismissively, not wanting to go into the detail.

"And when will they decide?"

"When they get around to it, I guess."

"So, the geologists will officially start the new epoch when they get around to it," Lilly chortles. "It must be nice to be so relaxed."

"Anyway," Rae says. "There's other reasons for having a fireball at the beginning of your calendar."

"Such as?"

"It saves you having one at the end."

Lilly looks up, her finger resting against one particular photo: an underwater nuke going off, on Bikini Atoll. The mushroom cloud is all white and surrounded by ships. She is going to ask after it but wants Rae to explain her last statement. "Say what?"

"Well, if you dig around in the soft flesh inside the head of a Western person, and sift through all the mush in there, you'll find nihilism & hopelessness. Most just accept that the world is going to burn-up some time in the near future. The Christians talk about Armageddon, and many of them actively work towards making it happen.

Forty per cent of the American public think that Jesus is coming back soon."

"Minus his foreskin," quips Lilly.

"Maybe he's coming back for his foreskin," says Rae.

They both laugh aloud and then look anxiously around the restaurant, concerned that they have been overheard.

"Let's not go there," Lilly says, authoritatively.

"Let's not. Anyway, other people worry about nuclear war. Those that follow science look at global warming and all flame that implies. A lot of people are convinced aliens have it in for us. And then of course, there's hell, fire and brimstone. So, on balance, most people think that the world is imminently going to get burned up."

"Yes, of course." Lilly studies the image of a W93, a nine-Megaton nuke resting on a trolley that is being towed by a yellow forklift.

Rae continues, "So, it is fixed firmly in the Western psyche that human civilization ends in flames sometime in the not-too-distant future. And that is hardly a worldview that lends itself to longevity for the human race. So, what Vita does, is it flips that on its head and sets the nuclear blast - the fireball, the heat, the flame and destruction - at the very beginning of the calendar. It is the primary event. And it leaves the end date unspecified."

"Don't you have a name for that?"

"The Long Future."

"That's right."

"It's conceivable that human civilization could be flourishing on this planet millions of years from now. But that won't happen while we have most of the humans wandering around convinced that we face an imminent Armageddon-like demise."

"The Short Future," Lilly says. "I think that it's very clever." She closes the book. "And I look forward to hosting the party and learning more about these fascinating weapon systems."

"Thanks for hearing me out." Rae seems both exhausted and relieved, having dumped all that information onto the table. "Anyway," she says. "It's so nice to catch up with my sister."

"Likewise."

"You've been away for a while, Lilly."

"I've been very busy. But I'm back now. And what about you, Rae? How's work?"

Rae shakes her head, anguished. "*Ughh*! Don't ask."

"Tell me. I want to hear about it. You seem anxious."

"I've been doing this environmental stuff a long time, Lilly. It's rare that something gets under my skin."

"Tell me."

Rae hedges for a while, but she's bursting to say it. "Look, I know that you are in the fossil fuel business, the conventional stuff. My sister is the Queen of Coal, after-all. I don't like that, but I've grown to accept that. The big issue with fossil fuels – as you may or may not be aware – is carbon emissions from burning the fuels. But there's this new fossil fuel extraction technique and it is just awful. I am so glad that you are not into fracking."

"Oh, right," Lilly says, glancing around. She has a sense of foreboding as to where the conversation might lead.

"Out of the blue, there is this new monster for us environmental people to deal with."

"Really?" Lilly asks. She searches for something to distract her from her sister's words.

"There is a huge hydraulic-fracking project destined for Central Queensland."

"*Ahhh.*" Lilly slides a menu from under the big picture-book on nuclear weapons.

"An American firm plans to drill tens of thousands of holes into the aquifers of southern central Queensland. It is going to destroy communities, ruin freshwater supplies and release millions of tons of methane into the air. It's awful. Awful. We are gearing up to fight, but with what?"

"*Uh-huh*?" Lilly says, nervously opening the

menu. Her eyes flit across the words, and she feels distinctly uncomfortable.

"We are not going to let this one go, Lilly. People are prepared to lie under bulldozers to stop this atrocity. Apparently, it is being funded by an Australian firm."

"Right."

"Have you ever heard of CH Fund?" Rae asks, directly.

"*Ummm,*" Lilly mutters, lost for words. She places a finger on the menu, "Oh, look. They have swordfish."

Quite a Bind

A few days later, Lilly sits in her lounge chair watching Alan and his mates continuing their work in the yard. A truck has delivered a mountain of turf. Two of the workers lay sod, while the others continue to uproot the roses, shake the mud free, and toss them onto the pile that will soon become a ceremonial fire celebrating the beginning of an epoch characterised by nuclear bombs going off.

Lilly hasn't made up to the extent that she normally does, and she is jittery. She hasn't been able to think straight since her lunch with Rae at Café Sydney. Her thoughts are clouded by the fears of imminent conflict, and pangs of guilt and self-consciousness. She is desperate to break through, and steel her nerves.

At the agreed time, Vinnie arrives, and Lilly pours an unhealthy measure of white into their glasses. She hands one to Vinnie, conscious of the fact that her hand is shaking. "I really am in quite a bind," she says.

"I can see, you are, poor dear. What's going on?"

"On one hand, I am soon to host the biggest event in the Vitan annual calendar. And on the other, I have unwittingly become their nemesis."

"The CH Fund?"

Lilly nods, anxiously.

"Just separate," says Vinnie. "Remember. Fat people sell health food. My dentist's tooth fell out."

"What?"

"I'm saying that you are an adult, Lilly. You need to put food on the table."

"I am worth over sixty million dollars, Vinnie," Lilly says. "I didn't do it because I was hungry."

"You did it because it had to be done." Vinnie ventures.

"I could have told Tom to shove the project up his ass."

"Well then you did it because that's the only thing that you know how to do," Vinnie tries again, hopefully.

"No. I am actually pretty good at sitting around doing nothing, Vinnie. You've seen me do that for years. I could have just kept doing that. I could even be doing Chrysalis Day, if I so choose."

"Well, then why did you do it?" Vinnie asks, perplexed.

"That's what I have been trying to figure out. I did it because that's what I do. It's Business as Usual for me. You listen to these Vitans talk, and it's all about 'not' doing Business as Usual. That's what caused the problem in the first place. And now it's caught up on me. And it's going to bring my house down."

"So, what are you going to do?" Vinnie asks, anxiously.

"Maybe I just do nothing."

"How will that help?"

"The CH Fund is waiting on my signature to open the trust account. Maybe I just don't sign it."

"Oh, really?" Vinnie looks distinctly put out.

"What's the matter?"

"I was going to come in on it."

"Oh, Vinnie! Forget the eight per cent, for a minute. There's something bigger playing out here."

"Like what?"

"Like I've never seen Rae in such a tizz. As soon as she started talking about CH Fund, it was like her world was falling apart. It was everything I could do not to tell her."

"Rae lives in a bubble. You've said that yourself."

"Well, so do I, Vinnie; a different bubble. And now my bubble is rubbing up against hers, and I'm afraid that hers will pop. She's my little sister. I can't have that."

"Oh, dear," Vinnie concedes. "You really are in a bind. And so, what happens if you don't sign it?"

"That's war with Tom Cata."

Vinnie perks up. "The divorce is back on?"

"I have been reading von Clausewitz," Lilly confides, feeling her confidence return.

"What is that? A thriller?"

Lilly shakes her head, and says excitedly, "He's a Prussian military strategist."

"Prussian?"

"His book 'On War' is read by officers in militaries all around the world."

"Why?"

"Why what?"

"Why have you been reading his book?"

"Just something that I picked up," Lilly says, brushing fluff off her leg. She glances across the room. The nuclear weapons coffee table book rests under a chair.

"And besides, war with Tom might be my best option, now. But how does one make the decision, Vinnie?"

"I don't know. Talk to your lawyer, maybe."

"Von Clausewitz says to weigh up two things: what you know will happen if you don't go to war, versus the uncertainties of going to war."

"I don't understand," Vinnie looks perplexed.

Lilly leans closer and explains, conspiratorially. "If I don't go to war - which is to say that I sign the contracts and kick off the CH Fund - a number of things are guaranteed. First, I will probably never get to speak to my little sister, Rae, again. She just won't talk to me, ever. Number two; I ruin my relationships with the Vitans forever. I become a pariah to them. And I like them. They are good people. And I will betray my understanding with Froyd Denison, such that one exists. And third; I unleash horrible consequences for the people and the environment in central Queensland. I have been reading up on this fracking, you see. I should never have got into this."

Vinnie nods, knowingly, a sufficiently grim look on her face. "I can see how that would upset you."

"On the other hand…" Lilly continues. "If I pull the trigger. If I don't sign the contract…"

"It's war with the Tom Cat."

Lilly nods gravely and sits back in her chair. She is lost for words for a few moments, staring into her wine glass for inspiration. "And the consequences of that are completely unknown to me."

"You'd have to come out guns blazing."

"Clausewitz talks at length about offense versus defence."

"What does he say?"

"I haven't read that chapter yet. But what I did read is this." Lilly leans forward again. "Because war is so damned expensive. If you are going to do it, get it over quickly. Short. Sharp and very brutal."

Vinnie steps of her chair and walks to the window. She puts her hand on her head, and watches the workers ripping up the final row of roses. "Didn't you just..." She shakes her head, and then returns to her seat. She holds out her glass and Lilly recharges it. "You should do it."

"You think so?" asks Lilly.

"Blitzkrieg. Is that the word?

"Lightning war," Lilly says, with a mean grin.

"Drop a bomb on the philandering bastard."

"Nuke him." Lilly says.

"Wipe him out."

"Pre-emptive strike."

"Burn him to the ground."

"I knew you'd agree," Lilly has an evil glint in her eye.

"Really?"

"Oh, yes," she says, excitedly. "That's why I asked you here."

CH Fund Contract

Shortly, an inevitable way point on the path to war is reached, when Lilly receives a phone call from Tom Cata. She looks at his name on the screen of her smart phone, and sets her jaw, gravely, as the phone rings, and rings, then rings out. She continues to watch the screen for the seconds that it takes for Tom to leave a message, and for the phone to respond with the notifying 'beep'.

She listens to the message. Tom is buoyant, excited even. He confirms the process as she had expected it. The lawyer has signed off on the contracts, Tom has signed the contracts, and all that is required to start receiving the pledged money and put the CH Fund into action, is her signature. The contracts are with the courier, on the way to her house.

Lilly lowers the phone and returns to her chair. She sits, pensively, for an hour, before she is alerted to the bell indicating that a visitor has arrived. Normally, she would buzz the courier into the grounds and sign for the documents on her doorstep. Today, however, she ceremonially trudges down the driveway and collects the package at the front gate.

Back inside her house, she lays the package on the sideboard in the lounge room. Then she retrieves from the drawer the manila envelope with the words 'Chrysalis Day' written on the front, in Froyd Denison's distinctive scrawl. She lays this next to the CH Fund package and stands back comparing the two.

She raises her phone and searches for the number of her lawyer. But she doesn't dial. Instead, she thinks it through. She doesn't need a lawyer at this point, she needs a strategist; someone who is smart enough to out-wit Tom Cata. Someone equally committed; someone with nothing to lose. Who is that? Froyd Denison, of course. Damn him from bleeding-out in the creek. She's on her own, this time.

To do this properly, she needs to gather a team, put as much though into annihilating Tom Cata as she put into setting up the CH Fund. She needs to set up a war room and bring in the right consultants and advisors.

If she is to do this and win, she needs to be clear on what winning means. What does von Clausewitz say about this? To win the war, you need to disarm the enemy, prevent them from fighting. But, what does disarming Tom Cata mean? If he were stripped of all his cash, he would probably bounce back, funded by people in his extensive network of the rich and powerful. How would she strip away Tom's reputation? Scandal. How hard would that be to do, the philandering old bastard? But then, the people who would come to his rescue are probably no different. How do you destroy the reputation of a rat to other rats? *Hmmm.* This is where the strategist comes in. Damned Froyd Denison. Where is he when you need him?

The War Room

Despite the absence of Froyd Denison to advise, Lilly gets to work setting up a place to plot her philandering husband's demise. Fittingly, she chooses the parking spaces for his two luxury sports cars as the War Room. She drives the cars into the yard, and in their place, sets up a large table with a black tablecloth. She strings a piece of rope and hangs sheets on this to separate the War Room from the rest of the garage. Once the basics are taken care of, she rearranges the items on the back shelf, trying to beautify the room. Next thing, she brings in some flowers in a vase, and sets these in the middle of the War Table. It is at this point that she realises that she has gone as far as her nerves will allow. Thinking about suing Tom Cata is one thing, actually doing anything about it, that's quite another.

She tries to put war out of her mind and concentrate on planning the Earth New Year party. There are nearly two hundred on the invite list, and there is much to be resolved: what to drink, what to eat, where to lay out the tables, the music, and where to park the fire engines, when they arrive.

Periodically, Lilly is interrupted by Tom calling on her mobile phone. There are international dial tones on his messages, so she knows that he is out of the country, and unlikely to visit any time soon.

The tone of his voice shifts with each call, becoming increasingly shrill, angry. He has a fearsome temper, and the crankier he becomes, the less nerve Lilly has in thinking through his demise. Soon, she is completely in denial about the consequences of not taking his call. She is not going to war, now; she is letting it come to her.

The closer the day comes to the party, the less she thinks about the looming conflict, and the more times Tom calls. She listens to each rant on the message bank, without really concentrating on the nature of his threats. In so doing, she fails to acknowledge that the latter messages are no longer accompanied by the international dial tone. Tom is back in the country.

On the afternoon of 16 July, Lilly sits in her favourite chair looking across the yard. The rose bushes, flown all the way from Japan, now form a pyramid-shaped mound, interlaced with logs and old hardwood shipping pallets, to really keep the fire going. There is a metal structure set up adjacent to the fire that is apparently to be used for the Gadget. The Gadget, whatever that actually is, is to be set off at exactly 9.29 pm, to coincide with 5.29 am in New Mexico.

Lilly draws the nuclear bomb coffee table book onto her lap and lays her hands on it as one might a lap dog. She continues to think through the evening, ensuring that nothing has been missed. She has considered the guests, the music, the food and grog – in abundance – the bomb-fire, the Gadget, the fire engines. What else could there be to plan for? Tom.

Tom Cata is likely to show at some point. What has she got in contingency for that event? Her phone rings and Lilly feels a shock run through her body. She checks the name on the screen and sees it is her drinking buddy, Vinnie. She lets Vinnie leave a message: that she'll be at the party around seven pm. As Lilly listens to the message, she looks at the hairs erect on her forearms. A million little soldiers stand tall, protecting her from the outside world. That's the extent of her army.

Earth New Year

It is dark outside, and the yard is filled with strangers. Lilly watches them from the kitchen. Rae arrives, flustered and excited. She wraps her arms around Lilly in a loving hug. "I am so proud of you, Big Sis," she says. "What are you doing inside?"

"Oh, I'm just preparing things, I guess."

"Come on outside. The whole community is here." She looks through the window at the revelry. Alan and his pals are taking care of lighting the bomb-fire, and the first show of orange flickers into life.

"Oh, wow!" says Rae. "I have never seen so many Vitans in one place." She takes Lilly by the hand and tows her through the laundry, to a spot where there is a commanding view of the party. Over two hundred people mingle, drinking, talking, and laughing. Compelling, psychedelic music floods the yard from a big sound system set up under a marquee.

"Who are they all?" Lilly asks, astounded, as she looks around at the bewildering array of Vitans. The crowd represent all shapes, colours, ways of dress.

Rae explains, "If you wanted to categorise them, they are Cultural Creatives, and Moderns in Transition. That's you, by the way – a Modern in

Transition. The people who aren't represented here are those who think everything is okay in society, or the people who want to go backward."

"Is that the common thread?" Lilly asks, bewildered.

"They all think that sustainability and happiness is important enough to work towards."

"That's it?"

"That's it. That's all it takes."

"Hi Rae," says an obese man, wearing a leather waistcoat and jeans cut down so far that part of his ass cheek is visible. He wanders into the crowd, where there is a cohort of similarly dressed men in a tight huddle.

"Hi Bear."

Lilly starts to chuckle, "Really?"

"That's Bear. He's a bear."

"Bears?"

"Large, hairy homosexual men."

"Of course."

"We have Vitan recruits from mainstream society and all the subcultures," Rae says proudly. "You see, if everyone who is progressive about something, becomes progressive about everything, then the system will shift, overnight."

"Is that so?"

Rae points out various individuals. "Over there,

drinking diet cola, that's the atheist Christian minister. You should have a chat with him; he's actually quite interesting. There are traditional Aboriginal people, over there. And over there, some ferals from the forest."

"From which forest?"

"From the forest on the other side of your wall."

"They live in this forest?" Lilly asks, alarmed. "But this is an elite forest."

"Funny. Anyway, over there are, some doctors and nurses. Those guys are musicians. That's the yoga group. That guy's a barrister. Those guys are monkey wrenchers. And those guys are cops. *Uh-oh!* Immiscible. I might have to keep those two apart. Excuse me." Rae wanders off, leaving Lilly to look at the social interactions taking place in her yard.

"I'll be inside," Lilly calls out.

"Okay."

When Rae catches up, Lilly is in the lounge room. "I've never seen any trouble at a Vita gathering," Rae says, "But then, I've always been pretty vigilant about keeping the immiscibles apart."

The house phone begins to ring, and Lilly turns towards it, her attention fixed. There's only one person that could be. She listens to answer machine repeat her message, then the 'beep' then the message.

Tom Cata's voice booms out, angrily, "Pick up, Lilly!" In the background, a humming noise indicates he is flying his helicopter.

"Is that your husband?" Rae asks.

"Unfortunately."

"How is Tom?"

"He's pretty cranky, right now. I'm fencing him on a project."

"Really?"

"Lilly. Pick up the goddam phone!" Tom yells into the answer machine. "The whole f**king project is on hold. We've got millions in pledges and no damned CH Fund trust account to put the money into. We need to f**king documents signed, Lilly!"

"*Hmmm.*" Lilly nods. No new information there. She looks towards Rae and sees that her younger sister has turned pale. She stares at Lilly, aghast.

"*Ahhh,*" Lilly overlooked something.

"The CH Fund?" Rae asks, her voice frail. "You are the CH Fund?"

Lilly glances at the floor, nodding slowly. She looks back to Rae, suddenly unsure of herself. "It's not going to happen. I won't let it happen."

"That's Tom Cata, Lilly. You don't f**k with Tom Cata. You told me that."

Hairs come up on Lilly's arms. This is the first

skirmish in the war, and she's fighting with an ally. Is this how it is supposed to work?

"I can't believe it," Rae says. She pulls her forearm around her stomach, grimacing. "My own sister." Her voice is strained. She looks at Lilly but sees right through her. "Why?"

"Why?" Lilly repeats. "I *ummm…* I guess I have yet to break with my own personal Business as Usual."

"Don't you see the contradictions?" Rae's voice is strained, like she is under intense pressure.

"But it's okay," Lilly says, unconvincingly. She moves to the sideboard, pulls open the drawer and retrieves the unopened contracts that are resting on the Chrysalis Day envelope. She holds the CH Fund contracts out for Rae to see, saying. "This is the contract that sets the frackers into action. I haven't opened it. I am not going to. I am not going to sign it."

However, Lilly isn't getting through. Instead, Rae's eyes are fixed on the contents of the open drawer. Lilly is perplexed, and she turns to see what her sister is staring at.

Suddenly, all the wind moves out of Lilly and she feels deflated and empty. She lowers the CH Fund package to her side and glances, mournfully, around the carpet. "Take it," she says.

Rae retrieves the Chrysalis Day envelope from

the drawer. "About f**king time!" she growls and moves quickly out of the lounge with the document.

Lilly watches Rae move into the yard. She accosts one of the guest and then points into the crowd. Panic flashes through Lilly as the thought comes to her mind, "Rae is sending everyone home!" The thought is too horrible to think. And yet, it is completely deserved.

It is so lonely standing on the top of the trench looking down, Lilly thinks. She is so terribly alone, now, feeling vulnerable. She ought to be covered in mud, in the Vita trench. Tattooed from head to foot. All over and all under. Instead, she has betrayed the Vitans. And Froyd. Or at least, she was on a pathway to betraying them. The betrayal only starts if the documents are signed. Assuming that the documents continue to exist, that is.

Her anguished thoughts are interrupted by a voice calling out. "Helloo! *Anyhoo*!" It's Vinnie. Just in the nick of time.

Lilly grabs Vinnie's hand, and tows her through the house into the yard, holding the CH Fund documents in her free hand.

"Where are we going? Vinnie asks.

"We are going to war."

"Do I have to come?"

The bomb fire in the middle of the garden is well

alight now. Big orange flames lap through the twisted jumble of rose bushes and shipping pallets. Lilly marches to the edge of the fire and holds the CH Fund contract above her head. She calls out to Rae. "I am going to do it. I will end the project right here."

"Whatever, Lilly," Rae says, unimpressed.

"This is my Business as Usual, going into the fire."

Rae marches over to her elder sister and berates her. "It really doesn't matter, Lilly."

"It must mean something."

"This movement is bigger than you, Lilly! It's bigger than your shitty fracking project, and your wealth!" Rae sneers, "This movement is bigger than climate change, itself! So just do whatever the f**k you want to do, Big Sis, because it really doesn't matter."

Rae moves away, and Lilly stands, stunned, the contract still held in the air. Her mouth is open, aghast. She has never had such invective targeted at her, not even by Tom Cata. She didn't even know it was possible for her sister to speak that way.

"*Uh-oh,*" says Vinnie, looking skyward.

The howling sound of a turbine engine approaches and the whoosh of air moved by propeller blades swirls around. Tom Cata swoops past in his black helicopter and turns to fly in a circle around the property.

Orange flame dances in the air from the former helicopter-denying rose bushes, now piled high. In their place are two hundred partying Vitans. They start whooping for joy, waving their arms at the helicopter as it moves overhead low and loud. Sparks erupt from the bomb-fire as the downwash fans the flames.

"Land over here," someone shouts.

"Oh, no. Don't say that," thinks Lilly. She looks into the cockpit, as the chopper passes, and sees Tom looking down at her. She becomes self-conscious, holding the CH Fund so close to the fire, and can sense that he knows what's going on. Tom shakes his head, gravely, and this puts a chill up Lilly's spine. She turns and marches towards the house.

"Holy-moley," says Vinnie, feeling out of her depth, as her friend departs. "I need a drink."

Return on Investment

In the kitchen, Lilly slaps the CH Fund contracts onto the table and stands there, wiping her hand down her face, trying to settle her nerves. Vinnie clips in behind, in her high heels. The sight of her shoes covered in mud cracks through Lilly's anxiety, and she bursts out laughing.

"What?" Vinnie asks.

"You don't have the right footwear for an Earth New Year party."

"Clearly not. And I am sober as a judge, too."

"Well, we can't have that."

Lilly whisks open the refrigerator that is crammed with every delicious thing to eat and drink under the sun. She selects a bottle of champagne and sets to work opening it.

"I'll get glasses," Vinnie clips across the tiles to the cupboard.

With bubbles in hand, the two friends chink glasses together.

"You're trembling again," Vinnie says.

"I couldn't go to war, Vinnie. I decided to let it come to me."

Just then, comes the sound of an angry voice as Tom Cata enters the house. "Lilly!?" he shouts as he swoops through the lounge room.

He bursts into the kitchen, catching Lilly off guard. His eyes fall to the package holding the CH Fund contracts. "I've been ringing, and ringing, and ringing and you've been screening my calls," he says, trying to compose himself.

"I am not going to sign it, Tom."

"Jesus!" Tom moves over to the cabinet and retrieves a glass, then pours it full of champagne. Vinnie steps back, unsure how all this plays out. She's never seen Tom agitated before.

Tom drains his glass in one slug, then grimaces as the bubbles flood into his nose. He turns to his wife and puts on his most charming smile and compelling argument. "Kitten. You spent two months putting this thing together. It's all but done. And it's worth a fortune. Can we…?" He draws the package towards him and unhooks the tear flap.

"Don't open that, Tom. It's not addressed to you."

Tom ignores her, tears the strip away and tips the contents onto the table. There are four bound documents with little pieces of plastic printed with arrows and the word 'sign', protruding from the side of the pages.

Tom flips a document open to the first page. He withdraws a pen from his pocket, hands it towards Lilly and sets his face with a stern glare.

There is the sound of commotion as a half dozen

people enter the building in the middle of a fast-flowing discussion. "Are we supposed to be in here?" asks one voice. "Why is there a helicopter parked in the street?" asks another.

The voices grow louder as the partygoers move along the hallway. They halt at the doorway to the kitchen, observing the tense stand-off. Lilly recognises one of them; the tall guy from Froyd's flux party. He's dressed the same: daggy old jeans and a rabbit fur waistcoat. Her eyes light up, and her response is the same.

"Lilly!" he says, surprised.

"Skun Rabbit!"

"Everything okay?" Skun Rabbit eyes Tom suspiciously.

"It's just fine," Tom snaps. "We're just going to finish some business, then Lilly can come out to play."

"Everything alright here, Lilly?"

Lilly inhales deeply. She looks down at the documents. She could sign them and have Tom out of her hair in seconds. A cramp takes over her stomach and her mouth goes dry. She glances up to see Vinnie shaking her head and this steels her nerves. She turns to Tom and says firmly. "Not now, Tom. I'm having a party." She turns towards the doorway to where Skun Rabbit stands, but before she can move Tom reaches out and grabs her upper arm. She swipes him away. "Get out, Tom!" she bellows. "I'll see you about this tomorrow."

"I don't know what the f**k is going on here, Lilly!" Tom directs the pen towards the people standing tensely in the doorway. "But you need to sign this thing right now."

"Leave it till tomorrow, Big Boy," says Skun Rabbit, taking a step forward.

"It's not your business."

"I'm making it my business," says Skun Rabbit, moving closer still.

Tom reaches forward, grabs Lilly roughly by the arm and thrust the pen towards her. "Sign the goddam contract."

Lilly swipes her arm, striking the pen from Tom's hand. He lashes out, slapping her in the face. Lilly shrieks and feels Vinnie take her by the shoulders and pull her aside.

Skun Rabbit moves on Tom Cata, grabs him by the shirt collar and delivers three punishing blows to the side of his head. *Bam! Bam! Bam!*

Tom falls, lands on one knee, clutching the side of his face, stunned. "What the f**k?"

"Three for one!" bellows Skun Rabbit. "Return on investment. Now f**k off!"

Tom gets to his feet, a palm pushed against the side of his face. "You're a f**king idiot, Lilly. I'll be back tomorrow."

Then, as if from nowhere, a champagne glass flies across the kitchen and strikes Tom squarely on the nose. Vinnie snatches up another glass and holds it above her head in the throwing position. She starts yelling: "Get out of here you philandering old tool! We know all about your dirty habits, you creep! You're on the divorce heap starting today! She's coming for you! She's coming for everything you have!"

One of the women in the doorway takes Lilly's hand and gently guides her out of the kitchen. "Let's get you some fresh air," she says.

Lilly holds her hand to the side of her face where Tom slapped her. Her skin aches awfully, and her head is spinning from all the action and anxiety. The kind stranger walks her out of the house, and Lilly turns to see Vinnie through the kitchen window yelling at the top of her voice, waving a champagne glass like it were a dagger. Good work, Vinnie! Personal protection force.

Lilly looks back to the huge bomb fire, and she starts laughing. The first casualties are coming off the battlefield, battered and bruised.

The kind lady hands her a drink. "That guy needs a restraining order."

"For starters," Lilly says.

A loud growling noise of a big engine comes

from the side of the house and a red flashing light pierces the night. Then a loud honking of a horn as two fire engines enter the yard. They are full-sized machines, glistening in the firelight. Alan and his mates direct them to their allotted parking spots while the firemen inside lean out the window waving to the people in the crowd.

Lilly laughs aloud. This is just ridiculous. Then from the other side of the wall, a black helicopter alights. The sound of the honking fire engines, the chopper and the party music all blends together into a mad cacophony.

Lilly sees Vinnie and Skun Rabbit moving in her direction. Vinnie is anxious and walking awkwardly as her high heels sink into the fresh turf. She wraps her arms around Lilly, "Are you okay, sweetie?"

Skun Rabbit places his big hands on her face and peers at the skin where she was struck. "You'll live."

"Thank you both for being my defence," she says humbly.

"It's not over yet," Skun Rabbit says, looking up at Tom's helicopter returning.

The chopper hovers over the bomb fire and slowly descends. The downwash pushes against the fire, sending it sideways and throwing embers into the air. The little orange chips of flame swirl around the partygoers. At first, it is taken as a game and the laughter and merriment increases. Then it becomes serious as the hot ashes stings someone's face. A woman starts shrieking, running around shaking her hands, her hair on fire. A big gust, and the hot wind washes over the crowd and there is a collective yell of panic. The firemen leap out of the truck and begin to pull out hoses.

"No way!" yells Lilly. She shakes her fist at the helicopter above. "You will not destroy this party." Then she breaks free of her companions and moves as fast as she can into the house. A minute later, she returns cradling a long, double barrel shot gun.

"Holy smokes!" says Skun Rabbit. He moves towards Lilly. "Do you know what you are doing?" he asks anxiously, holding his hand out to prevent her from raising the barrel above ground level.

"One thing about being raised in the aristocracy," Lilly says as she loads two cartridges of birdshot into the open barrels. "They teach you how to shoot." She cocks one barrel, raises the gun, and fires.

BANG! The sound of lead pellets striking the soft aluminium skin of the helicopter. The chopper wavers in the air, as if Tom knows that he is under fire and is changing flight plan. Lilly cocks the second barrel and fires again.

BANG! Pellets strike the acrylic canopy. Tom

turns the chopper away from the fire and drifts out across the forest.

There is a yell of excitement and cheers as two hundred Vitans get back to their party. The firemen stand down, and the driver of the fire truck repeatedly hits the horn.

Skun Rabbit takes Lilly's free hand, raises it in the air. Lilly raises the shotgun as high as she can, and Skun Rabbit shouts, "Victory!!!"

A loud cheer rings out across the yard in the mansion in the forest as the bomb-fire settles back into consuming the helicopter-denying rose bushes.

Skun Rabbit takes the gun from Lilly and passes her to Vinnie who has staggered up the lawn holding two champagne glasses.

"You did it girl," she says, handing over a glass. "You saw him off, big time."

Rae makes her way towards Lilly, the Chrysalis Day document in her hand. Lilly sees this and begins to tremble, uncontrollably. The champagne spills from the glass. She hands the glass to Vinnie, then reaches out for Rae. Rae takes her hand and they both walk towards the house.

Ecophany in the Kitchen

In the kitchen, Lilly breaks down. She becomes a mass of tears, barely able to stand. "I'm so sorry," she weeps. The trembling takes over her whole body. Rae places the Chrysalis Day document on the table and observes Lilly's meltdown with detachment and disbelief. Then she softens and cradles her elder sister. She wipes hair away from Lilly's forehead.

"I can't believe what I have been doing," Lilly trembles as she weeps.

"It's okay, Lilly."

"I have been fighting this all my life. I don't know why."

"Just let it in."

"I've been standing back, like Lord Muck, watching all the other people do the work. And what do I do? I set the monster free. Why would I do that?" She sobs, unable to breath properly. "You can't fight this on your own, Rae. You don't know what these oil people are like. They're so f**king mean."

Lilly clutches Rae and holds her tight. "Something has shifted in me."

"It's okay, Lilly. It's your Ecophany. You are just having Ecophany. It comes to all the good people, eventually."

Lilly lifts her head, wiping away her tears. "This planet is in a shit of a mess. So much misery and pain."

"Oh, yeah," Rae nods, wearily.

"Is there anything that we haven't messed up?"

"Not really, Lilly." Rae starts to chuckle, a cruel laugh.

"No?"

"Unfortunately, nope. Every ecosystem of scale has been tampered with or wrecked. The ocean is acidified. We're undergoing abrupt climate change and still burning billions of tons of carbon. Fisheries depleted. Topsoil washed away. The sea is choked with plastic. We've pretty much f**ked everything up. And that's just the environment." Rae runs her thumb down Lilly's cheek, removing a tear. "But look on the bright side."

"Is there one?"

"Sure, there is?" Rae says, cheerily.

"What's is it?"

"There's a lot of rich baby-boomers out there, doing just fine. So, there's that."

Lilly nods at length. She knows most of the ones who live on the Peninsula. "You need some rich baby-boomers working on your side," Lilly sniffs.

"You're not the first to make that observation."

"Are there any?"

"Not enough. It seems as though the richer they are, the rosier the world seems to them."

"What are we to do, then?"

"Well, I am going to take a look at Chrysalis Day. I am hoping that Froyd has written some magic in there."

"You haven't opened it, yet?"

"It wasn't given to me."

"Give it here." Lilly takes the envelope from the tabletop and rips it open. She tips the contents onto the table.

It is a single document, with the title: Chrysalis Day: Fostering Mass-Ecophany. There is a symbol, a stylised green horse, like some sort of Bronze Age art.

"There. It's done. Maybe you could brief me on the contents."

"Sure. You okay, now?

"Yeah. I am good now."

"Oh, by the way," Rae says. "I have a present for you."

"Does it have a nuclear bomb theme?"

"Some say that she is a bit of a bomb-shell."

"Kara?"

"Yes."

"She's here?"

"On her way. She's coming in from Perth for the night."

"Imagine, all the kerosene," Lilly says, chuckling and wiping tears.

"It's a cattle-class commercial flight, triple offset."

"So, he did it."

"What?" asks Rae.

"Froyd told me that he was going to get the Lord sisters back together again. Just for a night, at least."

"Let's see what this says," Rae says, raising the Chrysalis Day document. "Maybe it becomes permanent."

The Gadget

"What are you doing in here?" Skun Rabbit says, as he enters the kitchen. "They're counting down the New Year." He hustles Lilly and Rae into the yard.

Outside, Lilly checks her wristwatch and sees that it is 9:28 pm. For a moment she is confused, then she remembers that she is on Vita time, tonight.

The people in the crowd are chanting in unison, counting down the seconds to the turning of the year.

Lilly takes stock of the goings on. She sees that the firemen are in action stations. They have assembled into four teams with hoses locked under the arms. The man at the front of the hose has his hand clamped firmly around the handle, ready to turn on the water in the first instance.

"What are they expecting," Lilly wonders.

"Eight... seven... six... five..." call out the Vitans in the crowd.

"What's happening?" asks Lilly, taken aback by the energy of two hundred Vitans chanting in unison."

"Just look that way," Skun Rabbit points towards the metal cylinder on the other side of the bomb fire. There, Lilly sees Alan and his mates crouching behind a sheet of metal adjacent to the bin. One holds a red fire extinguisher. She can see that they are anxious and excited, about to set free the beast that they have been plotting in this yard for weeks now.

"Three… two… one."

A loud hissing sound comes from the metal bin. It rises in pitch and volume and then Alan shouts at the top of his voice, "NOW!"

There is loud rushing noise as two hundred litres of fuel grade ethanol doped with wood dust gushes into the air. Alan shoots an orange flame into the fluid and it catches, the rising liquid immediately engulfed in fire.

WHAAAFFFF!!

In a fraction of a second, there erupts an intense ball of flame, a pulse of burst of light and heat. Lilly gasps, and shades her eyes with her forearms. When she looks back, a second later, she sees a bright orange ball of fire that rises into the air. It seems to be half the size of the yard and looks just like the picture on the cover of the nuclear weapons book: sphere of bright orange flame, roiling and angry; the outside, dark and speckled with little chips of burning wood chip. The awful shape rises into the air with a dark stem sparkling with embers.

The crowd goes wild. Hollering and calling out. A fight breaks out in one corner of the garden and

Lilly watches Rae race into the fray. She pulls a whistle from her pocket and starts to blow, emitting a shrill tone.

The D.J. cranks up the music, a tune suitable to convey the spectacle of a mock nuclear explosion. The music sets the people in the crowd dancing.

The fighting boys in the corner of the year stop swinging their fists and hug each other, bouncing in time to the music. Rae wanders back to where Lilly, Vinnie and Skun Rabbit are standing. She is grinning broadly, shaking her head. "Vita Boys," she says.

"Come on Lilly. Dance." She takes Lilly's hand and walks to the place next to D.J.'s marquee where fifty people are bopping and shaking in the Earth New Year.

From the soggy patch of cold turf that functions as a dance floor, Lilly sees a group of five people enter the yard. They are flamboyantly dressed, like they have all stepped off a stage show - which they have. The petite one oozes energy like static electricity. She is slim, with a shock of black, frizzy hair. Lilly feels a tremor run through her; a tremor of joy - it's her little sister.

"Kara!" Rae calls out. She rushes across the yard and grabs her sister around the neck. Lilly stands back for a while, watching the pair of them hug it out. Then she moves towards her two younger sisters and drapes her arms around them both. The women sob, embracing for the first time in many years.

"How long has it been?" asks Kara, weeping. She rubs her cheek against Lilly's.

"Too long," Lilly says. "Far too long."

With the emotional embrace over, Lilly retires to the house to change into warm shoes. Rae steals Kara from her entourage and they huddle over the Chrysalis Day document. Shortly, they track down Lilly in the lounge room.

Rae holds up the Chrysalis Day document. She is about to speak when Lilly cuts her off. "We'll do it," she says.

"You don't know what it is."

"I don't need to. If it was invented by Froyd Denison, and will be executed by Kara and Rae Lord, then I want in, whatever it is."

After the Party

Next morning, Lilly wakes to see an unfamiliar sight. She is not in her room. Instead, she is on the couch in the lounge room. Wrapped around her, like the roots of a tree, are the arms of a man. She glances down, taking stock of the situation, and realises that one of his hands has penetrated her blouse and now rests against her breast. It is a most peculiar sensation, and not one that she is upset to be feeling.

Unfortunately, in this position, she is unable to determine who the man is, and hopes desperately it is Skun Rabbit, and not one of the ferals. She sniffs the air, detects a trace of patchouli oil, and sighs in relief.

She looks up to see her two sisters have entered the room and are standing there, grinning broadly.

"I never thought I'd see that," says Rae.

"Nor I," agrees Kara.

"What do I do now?" Lilly asks.

"Ask him his name." Kara leans forward to place a kiss on Lilly's forehead. "Thanks for a great party. I have to get back to Western Australia."

"When are you back here?"

"In a month. Then we'll catch up properly. And get to work on the Chrysalis thing."

Rae leans forward and kisses Lilly on the cheek. "Skun smells nice this morning," she says, winking.

The sisters depart and Lilly places her hand on the back of Skun Rabbit's and closes her eyes. She thinks back to the party, trying to recall the sequence of events that led to her sleeping with the man on her couch.

It's all a bit fuzzy. She remembers getting slapped by Tom Cata. Shooting his helicopter with a shotgun. Dancing barefoot on the cold turf. A huge mushroom cloud explosion. Drinking champagne from the neck of the bottle. Howling at the moon. Then smoking something in the lounge room.

Her eyes spring open. She will not have that material in her house! She takes Skun Rabbit's elbow and extracts his arm from her blouse. Then she struggles to extricate herself from the tree roots without waking the tree. Finally, steps up from the settee. She spends a few minutes searching the lounge for contraband, but it's not to be found.

Looking out the window, Lilly sees several people wandering around, picking up empties from the lawn and tossing them into piles. She wanders into the yard and says hello to the clean-up squad. It's two of the ferals. They are dressed in rags with dreadlocks in their hair. They have a distinct look and aroma of not having washed for a very long time.

"Hi Miss," says one. He's cradling a collection of empty bottles in the crook of his arm. "We've done the recycle collection for you."

"Well, thank you."

"Awesome party, hey?" he says.

From under a tarpaulin, there comes a voice, agreeing, "It was a really, really awesome party."

Lilly moves over to investigate. Five ferals have set up a rudimentary encampment out under a tarpaulin.

"There's enough food and booze left over to last a week," one says. "Do you mind if we stay?"

"You just want to stay there?"

"Is that alright?"

"If you like, you come into the house. Have a good hot tub." Lilly says, hopefully.

"Is that like a bath?"

"It is a very big bath. Lots of hot water, soap and bubbles."

"Soap?" The ferals confer on the matter for a few moments, and then one says, "We'll think about it."

"Very well, then." As Lilly turns away from the tarpaulin full of ferals, she hears the distinctive noise of a beer can crack open and a giggling noise.

She wonders what sequence of events made her

feel comfortable to have forest-dwellers camp out in her yard. A year ago, she would not have hesitated to call pest control and private security.

She checks the fire. All that is left of the helicopter-denying rose bushes is white ash. One of the big hardwood railway sleepers continues to smoulder. Its orange glow throws out warmth on the cold, winter morning.

The War Council

When Lilly returns to the kitchen, she finds Vinnie - who had claimed the larger of the spare bedrooms on arrival the night before - investigating the contents of the fridge.

"Look what I found," she says, holding up a pack of bacon that had been flown in from England for the event.

Lilly puts the coffee pot on the stove while Vinnie considers what would best accompany the bacon. When the coffee is brewed, Lilly goes to wake Skun Rabbit. She doesn't inform him about their sleeping arrangements, and he fails to mention it, so there is no cause for a difficult conversation.

When Skun wanders into the kitchen, Vinnie starts bragging about how she had taken the fight to Tom Cata the night before. "I told him good and proper," she says, boldly, "That Lilly Lord is coming for your skin. She's going to ruin you for good."

"I'm not sure that was such a sound idea," says Skun Rabbit, looking up from his coffee.

Lilly looks at him quizzically. That's an interesting comment. She thought that he was just handsome. Maybe he is smart as well.

"I mean, I don't know what the fight is," Skun

Rabbit continues, seeing that he has Lilly's attention. "But tipping of your enemy about your battle plan don't sound like something Sun Tzu would do."

"Sun Tsu," says Lilly, impressed.

"Sun who?" asks Vinnie.

"The Art of War. It's a book."

"Boy, you have a weird reading list," Vinnie mumbles.

"Come with me," Lilly says. She leads Skun Rabbit and Vinnie into the garage and pulls the sheets aside, ushering them both into the War Room. She sees the flower vase on the table with the black tablecloth and blushes as she moves it away.

"This," she says, spreading her arms to encompass the curtained-off space. "This is the War Room."

Skun Rabbit doesn't seem overly impressed, but Vinnie gets it straight away. "It's really happening?" she asks enthusiastically.

"It starts today. Who is on my war council?"

Vinnie throws a hand in the air, instantly. "Pick me!"

"Tactically, you are sound, Vinnie. And you are good for morale. But strategically, you can be rash."

Vinnie looks at the floor, nodding sombrely. "So,

am I in?"

"You're in."

"Yes!" Vinnie shakes a fist, a victory sign.

"Skun Rabbit?"

"I'm a bit lost here. So, what's the plan?"

"Let me explain," Lilly says. "My husband - who you kindly punched last night, thanks for that - is my sworn enemy. I intend to… crucify him; for want of a better expression."

"Why would you do that?"

"I have recently learned that he fathered a child to another woman while he was married to me and tricked me into spending millions of dollars to keep her quiet. As that money came out of a corporate trust account, that action potentially buys 'me' jail time. Fortunately, I have documents from the child – "

"Froyd Denison," interjects Vinnie.

"I have documents that proves his misdeeds. If I take the initiative, I can get my husband jail time. Furthermore, I have an agreement that half of the settlement from crucifying Tom Cata will go to the Vita Foundation. That's potentially tens of millions of dollars."

"Nice," Skun Rabbit, rocks nods at length taking it all in. He thinks it through but seems to get stuck on a point.

"So where does Froyd Denison come into this?"

"Vinnie," Lilly holds up a finger to stop her girlfriend speaking first. "Froyd Denison is my husband's bastard son; and by default, my stepson. He confided in me and gave me all the necessary documents to prove what I have said. I have confirmed them to be authentic. This was on the agreement that half the settlement from Tom Cata's estate - minus costs - goes to the Vita Foundation. I intend to honour that agreement."

"You want me to help you skin Froyd's dad?"

"Froyd wants you to help me skin up Froyd's dad," Lilly says, plainly.

"Now, that's very interesting," Skun Rabbit nods at length. Then he shakes his head. "You see, what I do, Lilly, I'm a timber getter and carpenter. I also catch feral rabbits - and the occasional cat - and make waistcoats out of their pelts. What you are talking about requires the services of lawyers, not a gamesman."

"I am not asking you to represent me," Skun. "I am asking you to support me. Help me make sound decisions."

"What did you have in mind?"

"Imagine that this house was a galleon, and we were going to take on the pirates."

"Sweet!"

"This War Room is the captain's cabin, and this is the chart table. Through there is the galley, always fully stocked. Upstairs are the bunks. The ship has at its disposal a full complement of highly trained crew, including consultants in all aspects of law, private investigations, public relations, security, banking and finance. I just need a few lieutenants around me to help me through it."

"I see."

"There's more."

"More?"

"There's lots more," says Vinnie.

"I'll pay a handsome salary. And if we win, Vita wins big time. Now, because we are going to war, it needs to be done hard and fast. Starting today."

"After a cooked breakfast," says Vinnie.

"Yes. After breakfast."

"This sounds like a Nicholas Monsarrat novel," Skun Rabbit chuckles, nodding enthusiastically.

"So, are you in?"

"Well, the rabbits won't miss me," Skun Rabbit holds his chin in his fingers, pondering it all.

"Are you in?"

"For Froyd Denison. Aye, aye, Ma'am. Let's go catch a pirate."

"Excellent," says Vinnie, scurrying off. "I'll get the bacon."

Planning Tom's Demise

Following a hearty breakfast, the drumbeat of war begins to resonate through Lilly Lord's mansion. Very quickly, the plan for the demise of Tom Cata takes shape. The War Room is extended to occupy the whole garage. Lilly's three cars are moved to the driveway, periodically accompanied by those of the consultants drafted in to help plan the battle. A disciplined routine settles into the house. Lilly leads, Skun Rabbit marches in lockstep by her side, and Vinnie fusses around, ensuring that the catering meets high standards. Work starts at 0900h sharp and ends at 2000h. Alcohol is consumed in moderation outside of these hours by Lilly and Skun, but in normal quantity by Lilly.

Skun Rabbit, having spent many years matching wits against rabbits and feral cats, proves to be an excellent strategist. He sets up a long whiteboard against the wall of the garage, and to this he pins photos, documents and post-it notes, all connected together with pieces of coloured wool. He has a natural aversion to computers, so Lilly maintains the digital library of documents and contacts. She draws up GAANT charts and critical pathways, and fires off dozens of emails every day.

Between them and the consultants, they map-out every conceivable alleyway that the wily Tom Cat might use to escape his fate. There is a snare set no matter which way he turns. It takes three weeks to design the strategy. Finally, there seems to be nothing more can be done except to shoot off some ranging shots, recalibrate, and then 'fire for effect'.

"Alright," says Lilly to Skun Rabbit, as the laser printer spits out the forty-page strategy document. "Let's go and talk to the lawyer."

"Which one?"

"The expensive one."

The expensive lawyer is in his early seventies. He specialises in divorce proceedings for wealthy people, and he only represents women. He says that he doesn't do the work for the money; instead, he does it because he is a staunch feminist. It's a compelling story, until you receive his invoice. The upside is that his success rate is second to none, and Vinnie has vouched for him on all of her three divorces.

The Lawyer's baldhead has a shiny patch that looks like as though it gets regularly polished. As the lawyer reviews a document on his desk, Lilly studies his head, convinced that she can see the ceiling cornice reflected there.

"Your case is very strong," he tells Lilly, looking up.

Lilly heaves a sigh. "When do we start?"

"Well, once it starts it won't be easy to stop. I'll have the papers drawn up and ready to serve on him in a few days. But before that, I recommend that you go to your husband with an ultimatum. Offer him an 'out', a way to save face. If that doesn't give you satisfaction, then call me and tell me that you'd like to begin."

Becoming Vitan

On the way back from the Lawyers, in the Bentley, the atmosphere is jovial. The nasty business of planning Tom's demise done and dusted for the time being. Lilly feels confident that she will be able to pitch Tom an out, and have the whole affair settled in no time.

Skun drives and Lilly daydreams, looking out the window, not concentrating on anything in particular.

"Is it hard to become an Vitan?" she asks, eventually.

"*Nahh.*"

"How would I do it?"

"Do you see yourself as a part of the Living Planet, and want to help advance the Verdant Age?"

"Two months ago, I would have said no, but now I say a resounding yes," Lilly says, solemnly after she has thought it through for a while.

"Right. You're in."

"Is that it?"

"Yep."

"That can't be it."

Skun glances over, curiously, "Why not?"

"It's too easy."

"It's not supposed to be hard. It's inclusive. We want everyone to do it."

"There should be a ceremony."

"Well, there is a ceremony of sorts."

"What's that?"

"It goes like this." Skun lets go one hand off the steering wheel and extends it. He closes the four fingers leaving just his thumb out. "One," he says. "The Long Future awaits, maybe."

"What is this?"

"It's your ceremony. Just follow along."

Lilly complies, holding her thumb out of a lightly clenched fist."

"Say the words."

"I can't remember what you just said."

"I only just said it."

"I wasn't concentrating.

"One. A Long Future awaits, maybe," Skun repeats.

"A Long Future Awaits, maybe."

"Good, two…"

"What does that mean?"

"It means that the humans could live on this planet a long time if we don't destroy things first. The Verdant Age is not assured. Ready?"

"Yes."

"Number two, natural living systems are sacred." Skun unfurls his index finger.

Lilly does likewise, repeating, "Natural living systems are sacred."

"Good. Three, happiness is a human right. Four, we are all in this together." Skun unfurls his pinkie finger. "Five, we are out of time."

Lilly follows along, completing with, "We are out of time."

"There," says Skun. "Is that ritual enough for you?"

"Is that it?"

"Memorise that."

"I already have."

"No, you haven't."

"Yes, I have," Lilly chuckles, indignantly. "Gee, you're cheeky."

"*Nahh*. You forget the first one as soon as I told you."

"I was bluffing. What do you call that, then?"

"That's the Five Fingers. You ought to memorise it."

"I already have."

"*Nahh*. Prove it."

"I'll prove you wrong." Lilly closes her fist, leaving the thumb extended. "A Long Future awaits, maybe. Natural living systems are sacred. Happiness is a human right. We are all in this together. We are out of time."

"Excellent. You can also say Long Natural Happy Together Time. Welcome to the Vitans."

"That's just a ritual. I want an initiation ceremony."

"An initiation ceremony? Why would you want that?"

"To formalise it."

"Why does it need to be formalised? I mean, if you cared about Bristlebirds, does that need to be formalised? Or do you just get on with caring for the Bristlebirds?"

"I guess."

"The trouble with formalising something, is that the process of getting formalised, sometimes replaces the actual thing being formalised."

"I hear what you're saying. I just won't feel like an Vitan without some sort of ceremony."

"Like what?"

Lilly is silent as she thinks it through. She is thinking of a Royal coronation in a cathedral. She once read a book on the ceremonies of the British Royals. She was enthralled with all the pomp and pageantry, all the trumpets and strutting horses. Maybe her ceremony could also include a national holiday.

Then, Alan the gardener comes to mind, standing outside her back door in his op-shop clothes. The diminutive man, who is always smiling, told her that caring for the Bristlebird simply meant leaving it alone. A coronation ceremony is exactly the opposite of what a Vita initiation ceremony would look like, she thinks.

"A tattoo," she says, eventually.

"A tattoo?" Skun asks, surprised. "Really? What of?"

"The horse."

"Horse?"

"The Ecophany horse."

"Where?"

"Same place as yours; on the nape. A little one, though. Down low, so I don't have to shave my head."

"I could do that for you."

"You could do it?" Lilly is pleasantly surprised.

"Sure, I could. I did Rae's tatt."

"Is that right?" Lilly is indignant. "Do all the Vitans get intimate with my younger sister?"

"It's not intimate, trust me. Getting a tatt is hard work."

"Okay, then. As soon as we get a payout from Tom; we'll do it then."

Meeting with Tom

The meeting with Tom is set in a restaurant in North Sydney a week later. Lilly arrives early in the Bentley with Skun Rabbit. She parks up, turns off the engine, and stares through the windscreen, her hands still gripped on the wheel.

"Are you okay?" Skun asks.

"I'd be lying if I said I wasn't anxious," she concedes.

"I'll come in. I'll sit at the bar," Skun offers. "Keep an eye on things."

"No. Thanks, but no. This is between Tom and me. I need to do it alone."

"And if he hits you again?"

"He won't hit me again."

"How can you be sure?"

"He knows he'll be jailed for it."

"Well, I'd be lying if I said I wasn't anxious," Skun slides off his seat belt, and cocks a smile.

They both laugh. Lilly lays her hand on his knee and looks in his eyes.

"Thank you," she says.

"He pats her hand in a friendly manner. "It's okay."

"No, I mean really, thank you. I have been procrastinating this for decades. Getting that man out of my life."

"I'll wait outside for you."

Inside the restaurant, the *Maître d* shows Lilly to her table, and she confides, "I am not sure how long I will be here or even if I will eat. Is that okay?"

"Today, everything is okay," he says as he pours water into a glass from a stainless-steel decanter. "Tomorrow, I'm not so sure."

The comment unnerves her, and Lilly elects not to raise the glass, uncertain whether her hand will shake and give her game away. She sees a shadow move through the frosted glass wall and recognises the gait of her husband.

Tom arrives, places a perfunctory kiss on her head, and takes his seat. He is smiling, calm. This is even more unnerving, than the *Maître d's* prognostication.

A tumble of thoughts comes to Lilly's mind. What does Tom think that he is here for? Maybe he thinks that she is going to berate him for slapping her, force an apology, and then get on with signing the CH Fund documents.

"I'd like to start with something, if I may," he says, right off the bat.

"Sure. What is it?"

"As a gesture of goodwill, Lilly. I forgive you for shooting my helicopter."

"*Uh-huh.*"

"Right, then. What are we drinking, today?"

"Just water for me," Lilly says.

"It's that serious, is it? Then, why don't you jump right in? I can see that something's eating you up. Are you f**king him, by the way?"

"What?"

"The guy who punched my head in your kitchen."

"Would it matter to you if I was?"

"Not in the slightest, Lilly. You probably should f**k him, actually."

"Well thank you, Tom," Lilly says sarcastically, stunned to be having the conversation so freely. She adjusts the position of a spoon on the cloth in front of her, noticing that her hand is not trembling. She takes that as a good omen and goes straight to the point.

"I have evidence, that in the time that you were married to me, while I was setting up Chartreuse Capital, that you fathered a child - Froyd Denison - to another woman."

She says this with her eyes fixed on the weave of the tablecloth. When she glances up, she sees that Tom has opened the menu and is nonchalantly browsing the reds.

"That's greenie bullshit," he says, running his

eyes down the list. “That little prick tried to blackmail me, too. I should have thrown him out of the chopper. I am frankly surprised that you fell for it.”

“I have all the documents, Tom. I’ve had them confirmed.”

“What documents?” Tom looks up from the menu, now alert. He meets Lilly’s eyes.

Lilly doesn’t shy away. “Tom, I haven’t come here to have a debate with you. I have come to give you a way out.”

Tom rests back in his chair. He runs a fingertip along his chin. “Give it your best shot, Lilly.”

“What I want from you, Tom, is three-fold.”

“Three-fold… What’s first, then?”

“I want a divorce.”

“Granted. What took you so long?”

Lilly is taken aback. What did take her so long? She has wanted a divorce since she first found out about his affairs. When was that? Twenty years ago. She is confused for a beat but pushes through. “Second, I want you to let go of the CH Fund. It’s finished.”

“*Uh-huh*. Well, I can’t move on that without you, anyway. So granted, by default, I guess. Three?”

“Yes. Number three,” she retrieves a piece of paper from her handbag. “I want you to liquidate half of your net worth and put the money into this bank account." She passes over a post-it note with BSB and account numbers written on it, and the words: Vita Foundation Ltd.

Tom starts laughing. "I love it." He takes the paper, folds it, and slides it into his breast pocket. "I'll get onto that, straight away, Ma'am."

"And I'll tell you why you should do that," Lilly says, firmly.

"I'm all ears."

"Atonement."

"What? Have I been a bad boy?"

"You are an asshole, Tom. You are a philanderer. You're a shallow materialist. You don't care for the people in your life. You spend your entire waking efforts in the service of the fossil fuel industry. You don't care about the environment. You are violent. Mean. Overall, you are despicable human being, and I think that gifting half of your wealth to the Vita Foundation goes at least some way to making up for that."

"So, you are noble and blemish-free?" Tom leans forward, as if to confide a secret. "You know that I couldn't have put that CH Fund together without you, Lilly? You know that don't you? Your skills are unique. Honed over years of doing exactly what I do. Investing in fossil fuels. Let me ask you a question."

"Alright."

"Are you selling up half of what you own, and contributing to this Vita fund?"

Lilly glances at the tablecloth, blocked in her advance. She nudges the spoon again, but it doesn't help. She feels alone and unprotected.

Tom slides his palm over the back of her hand and she is paralysed, unable to draw it away. "What the hell happened to us, Kitten? Do you remember France? How we drank and danced all night; and during the day, we plotted how to make a fortune. What a team we were. Where did that go?"

"With my money, Tom. How 'I' plotted to make a fortune with 'my' money, and 'my' strategy. You just mixed the cocktails, remember. I put my money into Chartreuse Capital. Now, I am taking my money out."

"You're pulling out of the fund?" Tom slides his hand away and sits back. "Is that what you are telling me."

"All of it."

Tom weighs it up, thinking through what the balance sheet will look like with Lilly's capital gone. It's not good, but he doesn't let on. A few seconds pass while he ruminates. He waves his hand, dismissively, "Sure. Whatever. What are you going to do instead?"

"Renewable energy."

"Renewables? F**k off!" Tom starts laughing. "The Government has been instructed to f**k that industry until it bleeds out. The volatility will kill you. You'll be broke in a year."

He turns away, his face red. He turns back, "F**king bullshit, Lilly! This country was built on base-load investment. You're the Queen of Coal. You know that."

"I don't like that name anym--"

Tom stubs his fingertip against the table. That doesn't satisfy his anger so he pulls the napkin from the table and shakes it angrily so that it makes sharp snapping noise.

"Jesus. There is a thousand years worth of f**king coal in central Queensland alone. Not to mention the gas, which you've decided is below you, now that you have your new friends. What are you even thinking? What do you know about renewables, anyway?"

Lilly raises a hand, conscious of the fact that she has lost the initiative. Tom will rant like this for hours if she lets him. He has made a good point, though. What does she know about investing in renewable energy – solar, wind, waves, tidal currents, geothermal power and sustainable biomass? Absolutely nothing, actually; but she will learn quickly, once Tom Cata is despatched. So, how is that crucifixion plan coming along?

"Kitten," Tom leans forward to take her hands again, but she shies away. "Kitten," he says again, imploring her. "If you want to play with these people, then play with them. You can f**k them; suck them; take it up the ass; whatever you like. Be the hostess with mostess, like the other day. You're good at that stuff. But do it *after hours*. And when you are being an adult during the paying time, don't give them your money. Don't give them our money. Don't take it out of the fund, Lilly. This low carbon economy stuff is just a bunch of f**king greenie bullshit. Don't buy into it. Please. For us."

Lilly starts speaking, quickly, seeking to get the information out, "Tom. I am not your Kitten. Not now. Now, I am you instructor. And this is your instruction. Go down the path I have laid out for you, otherwise I will…"

Lilly gulps. She is suddenly jammed up, unable to speak. She has only three more words that she needs to say but contained in those three words is the declaration of war. Is she ready for that?

She thinks back to her strategy sessions with Skun Rabbit, crafting the 'out' for Tom, some way for him to avoid ruin and to save face. Having him hand over half of his loot seemed like a good idea - when she was standing in front of the white board. Now she questions whether plotting against Tom

Cata with a rabbit-skinner was such a good idea. Now, the out just seems like a delusion. What the hell was she thinking? She ought to go back to the War Room and come up with a new plan. But with whom? Vinnie?

Lilly notices one of Tom's eyebrows rise slightly. He is trying to intuit what's going through her mind. He knows that she has an ultimatum, and that she can hurt him. The hush money from the trust account is damning, he knows. It could sink either of them, or both of them. It all depends on who starts the process first.

Lilly inhales deeply. She thinks of Froyd Denison bleeding out in the forest. He stood for something: sustainability, happiness, honesty, and integrity - the exact opposite of Tom Cata. But that's not enough to get her to say the final words. She needs a wedge, something personal. She places her fingertips against her cheek. Tom slapped her, in front of other people. He humiliated her in her own home. Her face begins to smart, as though her cheek were remembering the incident. She is not a Christian, who turns the other cheek. She's an Vitan. And if someone slaps an Vitan, they get slapped right back. Hard.

"Or what, Lilly?" Tom asks.

"Or, I'll take the lot."

The words just slip out of Lilly's mouth, like a

good idea whose time has come. She rests back in her chair, breathlessly waiting Tom's reaction.

Tom is motionless, staring at her with his mouth slightly open. She can sense the cogs whirring inside his head. Maybe he will conclude that she is bluffing, or unable to pull it off. Maybe he'll cave in, straight away. How many options are there? Has this been properly thought through?

Seconds tick by as Tom Cata stares across the table. As his calculus draws to a conclusion, Lilly sees a muscle twitching on the side of his nose, and she suddenly wishes that she'd okayed Skun Rabbit into the restaurant. Her stomach tenses, a subconscious reaction as she watches Tom's face turn noticeably red.

Then, swift and violent, Tom delivers a full-blown intimidation technique, its effect, instantaneous. He slams the side of his fists hard against the table.

CRASH!!!

Crockery leaps into the air, glasses shatter on the floor, and pieces of cutlery clang against each other. The noise is like a dropped piano landing hard. Around the restaurant, the normal white noise of chatter ceases, and all eyes turn to Lilly's table. The silence deafens.

Lilly's heart races. She is immobilized with fear, her eyes pinned wide open. Tom's face creases-up, and he leans forward so that his nose is just an inch from hers and he yells at the top of his lungs, "GET THE F**K OUT!"

Spittle strikes Lilly's face, and the hot, moist air from Tom's mouth washes over her with the scent of bad tooth; it's awful. In an instant, she's on her feet and moving quickly through the restaurant. She's not thinking, just moving on instinct. War has broken out in the restaurant. What would von Clausewitz call this battlefield tactic? Hasty retreat, maybe.

"Everything okay, today?" the *Maitre d'* asks, but Lilly carries on, without reply. She walks straight past Skun Rabbit who is resting against the wall outside the restaurant.

"Lilly," he calls out, and then chases after her. He catches up with her in a shopping mall and pulls her to a halt. She fumbles anxiously in her handbag and retrieves her smart phone, her hands shaking. She passes it over, saying, "I can't press the buttons, Skun. Can you call him?"

"Who?"

"The bald guy. The lawyer."

Skun does as instructed. He passes the phone back when the ringing tone sounds. The call goes straight through. She runs a hand down her face to remove the moisture, an amalgam of sweat and Tom Cata's spit.

"Hello… Yes... This is Lillian Lord... As you suggested, I talked to my husband... I didn't get satisfaction… And I would like to begin."

Stop Pacing

Back in the War Room, Lilly paces back and forth, scratching her scalp. Round and round she goes. Skun Rabbit rests back, calmly watching her. He thinks that Lilly's reaction is reasonable, now that she has gone beyond the point of no return.

Vinnie clucks around flustered, asking the same question over and over, "What do we do now? What happens next?" This only serves to make Lilly pace and scratch harder.

Skun chuckles, realising that there is only one way to regain some semblance of sanity. He departs the War Room for the galley and returns with a bottle of champagne and three glasses.

He pops the cork, pours the glasses and lays them on the table. Lilly stops pacing. She shakes her head, coming to her senses. "I still have the smell of his breath in my nose," she says.

Skun moves over, "Come here. Close your eyes."

Lilly does as instructed, and Skun places his hand around the back of her head, and gently moves the champagne glass to her face so that the rim is just under her nose. "What do you have in your nose, now?"

"Fruity bubbles," she says.

Skun moves his index finger, tickling her nape. "This is where your tattoo's going, when this is over."

Lilly places her hand over his wrist and stays that way, breathing in the aroma of the champagne and feeling the energy pulse from the wood-cutter's body into hers. "I thought that you said it wasn't intimate."

Skun chuckles, "Just wait till the needle starts."

Now Vinnie starts to wander around in a circle anxiously, almost like she was willing the champagne treatment for herself.

"I've got a project that would be excellent for you, Vinnie," Skun says.

"What's that?" Vinnie asks, as she refills her glass.

"We are going to run interference on Tom Cata."

"I am not leaving this house until that man is in jail," Vinnie says, firmly.

"You don't need to. There's a city full of Vitans out there. Your private investigator and his team can tell us exactly where Tom Cata is at any moment of the day."

"What are you suggesting?" Lilly asks, her eyes still closed.

"It's time that we unleashed the Vitan Ninjas."

Vita Ninjas

Vinnie takes to her new role with aplomb. She is the liaison between Chad Thompson, the Private Investigator and Skun Rabbit who runs the Vitan Ninjas.

The PI's role is to provide minute-by-minute updates on Tom Cata's movements. When he goes to a coffee shop, Vinnie learns how many sugars he has. When he parks his car, Vinnie knows which car park and which bay.

She briefs Skun Rabbit on these details, and Skun makes calls seeking Vitans in the vicinity.

"He's at the coffee shop in Bellevue Hills, Vinnie reports, putting down the phone to the PI. "He's having a flat white and a danish."

"Excellent, there's a Vitan waiter there. Let me make a call." Minutes later, the P.I. reports back that someone has spilled a tray of soft drinks down Tom's front; by accident, sort of.

Next, Vinnie learns that Tom has parked his car on the roof of Westfield Shopping Centre at Bondi Junction. "He's in Rodd and Gun buying a new shirt."

"Well, that's good. There's an Vitan works in building maintenance," Skun says. "I'll give him a call."

Shortly the P.I. reports back that Tom is shouting

into his phone to the Royal Automobile Club who has informed him that they will be delayed getting to him, to inflate his four flat tyres.

"Four flat tyres?" Skun asks, surprised. "Good work."

Hours pass with Tom Cata sitting in the car park waiting for the tyre pumpers to come. The P.I. calls back with news. When the tyres were finally filled, and Tom drives away, he finds that his bumper bar has been tied to the steel rail.

"So, he drove off without the bumper," Vinnie says.

"Good news," says Skun Rabbit. "This puts us into a whole new ball game; a vehicle offense. Now, Vinnie, did we get that little package of white powder into Tom's glove box, as requested?" Skun Rabbit asks.

"That went in last night," Lilly confirms.

"Well, that's great news," Skun says. "Time to call the constabulary."

Shortly the news comes that Tom has been pulled over by the police. Next, the P.I. reports that his car is being searched. Next, the P.I. reports that Tom Cata has been handcuffed and pushed into the back of a police car.

"Okay," says Skun Rabbit. "Good work, let's get the Ninjas to pay a visit to Tom Cata's residence."

When Tom Cata gets home from the police station lockup the next morning, he is still sticky from the cola spilled in his lap. He is in a foul mood, which only worsens as he stands in the hallway, bewildered.

Where the hell is everything? The entire building has been stripped bare. Everything is gone. Furniture. Valuables. Paperwork. Passports. Even the legal documents from Lilly's bald lawyer are gone. Also missing is the preliminary briefing from his lawyer regarding the charge sheet laying out twenty-six counts of securities fraud and breaches of the Corporations Act. According to Tom's lawyer, he needs to keep a very low profile and squeaky-clean. If not, he faces significant, jail time."

"What the hell?" Tom asks aloud.

He is alerted to a flashing light. The one remaining item in his home is an answering machine sitting on the carpet. He slaps the toe of his shoe on the device, activating the message. He recognises the anxious voice of the manager of the airfield where his helicopter lives. "Tom. I'm really sorry to give you this news. Last night, someone stole your chopper."

"F**k!" He stomps his foot repeatedly on the answer machine until the airport manager stops talking.

Then, there is a knock at the front door, and Tom

stops stamping on the answer machine. Strange. He doesn't get visitors at this home. He moves cautiously to the door and peers through the eyehole. Outside, there is a large, obese man, holding a mobile phone in one hand, and a sports bag in the other. It is Bear, the bear from the Earth New Year party.

Tom pulls open the door, ready to start shouting or punching as need be. However, despite being a Taekwondo brown belt, the Bear doesn't have any aggression about him.

"Mr Lord," Bear says sweetly.

"Who the f**k are you?"

"Just the messenger, sweetie." Bear passes over the mobile phone and the sports bag. "Enjoy Brazil, you lucky boy." He turns and walks away.

"What?" Tom places the phone against his ear, confused.

Lilly's voice is light and carefree. "Hi, Tom."

"Lilly?"

"This is your out, Tom. It's your last chance. Can you hear me?"

"I hear you."

"In the bag are some fresh clothes and your passport. Plus, there is cab fare to get you to the airport and a ticket, one-way to Sao Paulo, Brazil to see your little girlfriend. It's a cattle class seat, and it's not a direct flight. I went looking for the best price, you see. You do realise, of course, that if you leave the country with all these charges piled against you, that you won't get back in without being arrested at the airport. So, if you decide to go, you're gone for good."

"You've taken everything from me," Tom mutters, aghast.

"Not yet Tom. That's next. And besides, you have plenty stashed away in Brazil. You won't be hungry."

Tom's Gone

An hour after the call with Tom, Vinnie takes a call from the P.I. who says that he has followed Tom to the international airport and that he has checked in and carried his hand luggage through security. He asks what he ought to do now.

"I think that we can send the Private Investigator home, can't we?" asks Vinnie.

"I think so."

Next, Vinnie calls the bald lawyer and shares this news with him.

"That should speed things up considerably." He tells her.

With Tom on the flight to Sao Paulo via Hong Kong, London and New York, Lilly calls an extraordinary board meeting of Chartreuse Capital.

She rings each of the Directors personally in the small hours, instructing them to the boardroom for 10am. She tells them that Tom has skipped the country to avoid legal proceedings relating to fraud and that she is taking over the reigns of the company.

When the Directors arrive, they see Lilly seated calmly at the head of the table, and a stern-looking woodcutter standing behind her, silently, with crossed arms.

In front of each of the seats around the table is a stack of printed documents with plastic tabs highlighting relevant pages.

Once the Governors are seated, Lilly calls the meeting to order, and begins. "As per Clause 44b of the company constitution - that's tab one, by the way - in the event of the Chairman being placed under criminal investigation, Mrs Lillian Lord takes over as Chair of Chartreuse Capital. As you will see – tab two – the Chair's role includes hiring and firing directors." She looks around at each of her directors observing their discomfort and confusion. She lets them sweat for a while before finally announcing,

"Let's say that I wanted to have conversation about climate change in the board room," Lilly says. She is met with a derisive chuckle from most of her board members.

"No? Has there ever been a conversation about climate change in the board of this fossil fuel investment house?"

One of the Directors, Sid McKeon, answers in his usual long-winded manner, "Certainly at a board level that's not a particular question that's ever been on our agenda, Lilly."

"You just don't talk about climate change in the board room, do you?" she asks.

"You know this, Lilly. You read the minutes."

"It was a rhetorical question, Sid."

"No one talks about climate change in the board room in this country. And I wouldn't want to risk us being the first."

"Risk averse. Thank you, Sid, I appreciate your candour. I draw your attention to document two. This is a copy of an article from the Australian Financial Review announcing the passing of the Paris Accord, that seeks to limit anthropogenic climate change to below two degrees above the industrial baseline. Did anyone have a conversation about this, at board level."

"No, Lilly. No one did. Not in this board, nor in any board in this country, I dare say."

"Very well then," Lilly says, formally, her suspicion confirmed. "The following people: Sid McKeon, Tom Firth, Cassandra Drew, Leo Salt, and Nick Lewis," she looks up and glances around the table. "All present. You're fired."

"For what?" asks McKeon, indignantly.

"Incompetence. I refer you to clause…" Lilly is interrupted as the five Directors stand angrily.

"Bullshit," growls McKeon. "We'll get Tom back to sort this shit out. How long have you been plotting this hostile coup?"

"I figured that I might need to mow the lawn one day, Sid. Twenty years ago, when I was writing the constitution."

"Would you care to leave the room, now, please," says Skun Rabbit, moving forward.

"Why is there a lumberjack in here?" asks McKeon as he is ushered out the door with the others.

Once the five directors have departed, just two remain. Carol Burnett is a vivacious redhead, and Teddy Lang, a studious man with thick glasses. They both look to be in a state of shock.

Lilly pours two glasses of water and passes them over. "From this moment," she says. "Chartreuse Capital is charting a new course in renewable energy investment. You've had eight hours to think it through. Carol?"

"About bloody time, Lilly. We'll need to manage the PR very carefully so as not to spook the investors."

"Agreed. Teddy?"

"Lilly, this is not something you do quickly. Even the analogy of turning a ship around is not adequate."

"What's it like then?"

"It's like turning a ship into an aeroplane. The yield profiles, risk profiles… Everything is different."

"So, are you with us?"

"Absolutely. In the first instance, we'll need to

replace the fund managers. Maybe even the CEO."

"I agree," says Burnett.

"That said," continues Teddy. "With a steady hand on the helm, I think that we could keep most of the investors onside and get out of fossils and into photons in twelve to eighteen months. After-all, the investors are with us for yield, not for fossil fuels, *per se*."

"That's exactly right," Burnett says, enthusiastically. "And because we haven't been talking about climate change in the board room, we haven't been talking about climate risk. Un-burnable carbon and the carbon bubble are known-unknowns for this company - huge, unacknowledged risks. The whole industry in this country is in denial. If we have fund managers who understand how the Paris Agreement affects fossil fuels versus renewables, we'll have a huge competitive advantage, and it won't be hard to make an argument for change to our investors."

"And we wouldn't be the first," says Teddy. "There's a lot of international precedent to show that this strategy works. There's a huge divestment movement already underway. Trillions of dollars moved away from fossil fuel investments."

"Good," Lilly says. "This is what I wanted to hear. So, moving forward, what's next?"

"We need to get a press releases out today. We

should get you on the TV. Lateline Business," Carol says. "We need to break the news before anyone else does. Explain why the Queen of Coal is divesting from fossil fuels."

"Well, that's easy," Lilly says, lightly. "Chartreuse is a shade of green, after-all. And I never did like being called the Queen of Coal. The Regent of Renewables, maybe…"

The door of the boardroom opens, and a suited man enters. The CEO looks around, confused. "I was told to come in on a board meeting."

"Come on in. Sit down," Lilly says. "This is your new board."

"And Tom?"

"Tom's gone," says Lilly.

Chrysalis Day HQ

With the company set on a new course and Tom out of the country, Lilly's is finally free to concentrate on the pressing matter of Chrysalis Day.

She talks this over at length with Skun Rabbit, and they come to the agreement that rather than renting office space, the mansion can become the headquarters of the program.

"If this house is to be Chrysalis Day HQ, I suggest a refurbishment," Skun tells her.

"You don't like the colour?"

"I'm more concerned about the carbon footprint."

"What do you have in mind?"

"I have a list here." Skun retrieves a notepad that has page after page inked with his distinctive handwriting.

"That's not a list. That's a tome."

"There's a lot of work to be done. Starting with ditching about four hundred halogen lights, replaced with LED."

"I don't know what that is, but it sounds like you do."

"Next is the solar PV on the north facing roof, which will be painted with solar reflective paint, by the way."

"That's a designer roof," Lilly grumbles.

"We'll get designer paint."

Skun continues to read off the list, a complete eco-efficiency retrofit. He concludes by saying that the house will become a net exporter of energy and a carbon sink.

Lilly is not versed in this new language, but she is confident that it is what an Vitan would do. Her mind drifts off to her sisters.

"Kara's back in Sydney next week," she says, smiling.

"That's great news," Skun adds another item to the eco-efficiency wish list.

"Yes, and as per Froyd's plan, as soon as the three Lord sisters are together, we'll get to work on Chrysalis Day."

Cirque du Soleil of Sustainability

The air is warm, the sea calm and cobalt blue. The long, sandy beach stretches ahead. In the distance is the Barrenjoey lighthouse on the rocky headland. The three Lord sisters walk along Palm Beach. Lilly lags behind Kara and Rae as they chat.

"I was diving on the Great Barrier Reef last year, and now I hear that it's all gone," Kara says.

"It's not all gone," Rae replies, "But it's on its way."

"Why is that happening?"

"Heat, mainly," Rae tells her. Most of the heat trapped in the atmosphere ends up in the ocean. And everything is stressed. Not just the coral. We've lost 40 per cent of the phytoplankton in the last fifty years." Rae halts. She teases an empty shell out of the sand, and then flicks it along the beach.

"Do you understand what that means?" she asks. "To have killed off half of the plants that produce the oxygen we breathe. That's not just a statistic, anymore. That's a profound insight into humanity's spiritual relationship to Mother Earth."

"I get that," says Kara, nodding. "It's a spiritual issue."

"Exactly. And if we humans want to claim that we are superior to other organisms, we can't be doing that," Rae continues. "Otherwise, we are just as good as a bug. Worse than a bug, actually; at least the bug has a function. The only way to see this is that we humans have a role on Earth, to protect the Living Planet and to foster happiness. We're just not doing our job, yet."

"No one ever told me that," Kara says. "If people aren't doing their jobs, maybe it's because they haven't been told what their duties are. What's the first job?"

"We have to stop burning fossil fuels and suck huge amounts of carbon out of the sky."

"Can we do that?" Kara asks.

"Technically, yes. But we are desperately short of time."

"That's the little pinkie finger," Lilly says, waving her finer in the air.

"That's right. One of the Five Fingers. Plus, it requires the full co-operation of governments and industry."

"Aren't they both sort of controlled by the public?" Kara asks. "With the elections and the things that people buy?"

"In theory, yes. But that requires the pubic to be doing their job. And in order to get them to that, we need to get them to wake up."

"Ecophany," says Lilly.

"That's it. So how do we foster Ecophany, on a

big enough scale to make up for the lack of time?"

"Well, this is what I am good at," Kara says, striking the air with her fist. "Getting the public to do things, like, smile, be happy. Visit my website. Listen to my podcasts. Get involved. Buy a ticket. Get into the funnel."

Lilly steps in, "And that is exactly what Froyd Denison had in mind with his Chrysalis Day plan. What you do, Kara, focussed on sustainability and happiness, but done on a grand scale."

"Well, that's easy. I just need to create the new content."

"How do you get your content?" Rae asks.

"Well, Happiness in Hyperdrive is all based on psychology. I get psychologists to advise me. I listen to what they say and translate it into a form that the public can resonate with. You are the subject matter expert on sustainability, Rae. So, together we'll weave together a new story that the public will be gagging to hear. What's the core message?"

"The planet's dying, and it needn't be," Rae offers.

"I'd say the positive. *The planet could be made healthy, again.*"

"Is that where I've been going wrong," Rae chuckles.

The blue ocean laps against the sand beach with a melodic tune, a rush and a crash repeated over and again. Overhead, seagulls and terns hover on the breeze, studying the beach for food. In the distance, the headland of Barrenjoey is an amalgam of brown rock and green vegetation. Lilly, listens in on her younger sister's discussion, can't help but feel as if the lighthouse up ahead is a deeply symbolic beacon. Her whole life, she now understands has been in direct conflict with her innate responsibilities as a human being: to nurture the planet's life support system, and to help foster contentment amongst other people. Now that she has had this insight, it cannot be unseen, it cannot be unthought. She feels like the insect described in Froyd's document, Chrysalis Day, she feels as if her whole life has been a caterpillar, and that the past few months she has been metamorphosing inside the chrysalis and is now free to stretch her new wings in the sun.

Kara continues, "If you want to enrol an audience of strangers who are not familiar with your subject matter, you have to speak in curves. That's my speciality, finding and presenting the curves. Try this…"

Kara strikes a pose and projects her voice from her diaphragm, "With care and affection, our planet could be bought to full health!"

Lilly is taken aback at how much energy emanates from Kara's tiny frame. "Heck!" she says. "That'll do it."

"That's a great message," says Kara, excitedly. "Sustainability is a natural complement to happiness. You look inside for happiness, and outside for sustainability. Happy people, happy planet."

"That's Chrysalis Day," says Lilly. "How long will it take you two to put it together?"

"I am ready to go." Rae says. "How long does it take? She asks Kara.

"Six weeks to write and rehearse new content. It takes a lot longer to perfect it, though. I have only just nailed the Australian performance and we're at the end of the run. I reckon we go back around Australia with the new content. It will be perfect by the time we've done that."

"How long does that whole cycle take?" asks Lilly.

"About six months."

"*Uh-huh.* By that time we'll have an international marketing plan and a budget. Plus, we should have Tom Cata's cash in the bank, too. What are your margins in this business?"

"The public pays over a hundred dollars a ticket. But the promotional costs are huge."

"How much are you spending on promotions?"

"Thousands," Kara says.

"What if you had millions?"

"That's a huge show," Kara says. "That's an international show. I'd need ten of me, for that. Twenty. No, that's a completely different model."

"How so?" asks Rae.

"Well, my current model relies on the panache of the presenter – that's me – to engage the audience. But you can only do one show a night. If you want to spread this message around the world and quickly, you need a new model. Is that what you want to do?"

"That's what Froyd wants to do," Lilly says.

"Screw Froyd." Rae says abruptly. "He's in the flux.

Suddenly, Kara starts hopping around, clapping her hands together. "Yes. Yes. Yes. Yes. Yes," she chants, as she spins around in a circle, on the sand.

"I love it when she does this," Rae says.

Kara comes to a halt, her face alive in excitement. "This is what I have been aiming for, all along. But I thought that it would take years to get there."

"What?" asks Lilly.

"With the Chrysalis plan, we can go straight there! This is…" she pauses, thinking it through. Then she draws her hand through the air in front of them, for effect, "The *Cirque du Soleil* of sustainability."

"Yes!" shouts Rae, excitedly.

"We use their model. They don't just have one show. They had dozens of shows. The permanent shows in Las Vegas play to nine thousand people, a night. Nine thousand a night!"

"No way!" Rae exclaims, stunned. "Imagine if we could foster nine thousand ecophanies a night in one city. That's Mass-Ecophany!"

"And that's just one city," continues Kara. "They reckon that over ninety million people have seen a *Cirque du Soleil* show."

"Ninety million!" Rae says, aghast. "That starts global spiritual revolution."

"Is that what you want?" asks Kara.

"That's what all the Vitans want," Rae says. "Hell, that's what the planet wants."

"So that's the plan, then," Lilly says. We design a show that can be replicated as many times as possible."

"I'll advise the content," Rae says.

"I'll train the presenters," says Kara.

"I'll manage it," says Lilly. "And Tom Cata will fund it."

Tom's Gone Feral

When Lilly returns home, she finds Skun Rabbit standing in the hallway, holding a cardboard box full of incandescent lamps. In the corner is a pile of empty boxes that had recently contained LED lights.

"How's the retrofit coming along?" Lilly asks. Skun doesn't reply. He just stands there with a grim look on his face. He shakes his head slowly, indicating that he is having trouble forming words.

"What?" Lilly asks, now, concerned. She takes the box from Skun's hands and places it on the floor.

"What's going on, Skun?"

"I was checking the cat traps in the forest," he says.

"Okay. And?"

"Put your boots on, Lilly. You need to see this."

"Can't you just tell me?"

"You really need to see it."

Lilly follows Skun down the yard and out through the iron gate. He moves quickly through the forest, following a path through the undergrowth that is barely visible. Lilly struggles to keep up and finally, a kilometre from the house, they come to a rocky outcrop where there are signs of human habitation.

Skun tells her. "This is a feral encampment. They

live in the caves."

"Yo!" he calls out and there is movement. A half dozen dirty faces peer out of the shadows. Lilly recognises them from under the tarpaulin on the morning after the Earth New Year party.

One face she recognises from somewhere else.

"Tom?" Lilly asks, astounded. She takes a step forward.

"We found him in the rain outside your gate," says one of the ferals. "He didn't look happy, so we took him in."

Tom is wearing a ruined suit, the one that Lilly packed into the gym bag for him. He is filthy, emaciated. His fingernails are encrusted with dirt. His clothes are ripped and damp. He crawls forward on his hands and knees. The tears pouring down his face create two clean streaks on his filthy cheeks. "Kitten," he implores, holding out a hand.

"Don't Kitten me, damn you!" Lilly snarls. She takes a step forward and Tom withdraws. He curls up, holding his hand in front of his face.

"Don't do this to me, Lilly. You're all I have."

"I am all you had, Tom. You lost me a long time ago. I was creating something for us. And you were f**king around."

"I'm just a little person, Lilly."

"You should have just gone to Brazil."

"There is nothing there for me, Lilly."

Lilly turns to Skun Rabbit, a confused look on her face.

"You need to finish this now," he says. "Otherwise, it will keep biting you."

Lilly nods at length. She turns to Tom, "What are you even doing here?"

"I wanted to see you. So, I came here. It started raining. Then these guys found me."

"You've been here for two weeks?"

"I'm starving, Lilly. I'm so cold. Give me another out, please. I'll take it, this time."

Later that evening, Lilly and Skun are seated in the lounge room. Lilly sees movement reflected in the bay windows. She turns to see Tom standing in the room. He is wearing the bathrobe and holding a crystal tumbler containing a gold-coloured spirit and big chunks of ice.

He says with a humble tone, "That bathtub is incredible. Thank you, Lilly."

"You are welcome, Tom. Sit down. Did you eat?"

"Thank you. Yes."

"Your clothes are on the end of the bed."

"Thanks," Tom sits, adjusting the bathrobe. "This is beautiful fabric." He motions towards the bathrobe.

"That's Quitlan Mare," Lilly says, feeling like she has had this conversation once before.

Tom glances nervously at Skun. Skun winks in a friendly manner, and Tom nods his appreciation.

"I have drawn up a contract for you," Lilly taps a pen on the notepad on her lap. "If you sign this, we'll get you back into your life tomorrow morning."

Tom takes a sip of whiskey and rolls it around his mouth. And if he doesn't sign it…

Lilly will press hard, he will lose everything, and probably go to jail for a decade. He nods pensively, desperately hoping that this 'out' leaves him with enough to maintain his dignity. He has been Lilly's business partner for over two decades. But this is the first time that he has actually been 'the business.'

"Are you ready?"

Tom nods, gravely, his stomach tight.

"Tomorrow morning, you will transfer your entire holding in Chartreuse Capital to the Vita Foundation." She refers to a printed document. "That's about one hundred and twenty-five million, at current market price."

Tom continues to nod, anxious for what comes next. "You can keep your cars, you helicopter, your house, and its contents. And as for the three cash accounts totalling five million, you can keep that, too."

Tom eases a huge sigh of relief, almost sinking into the dressing gown. Lilly hands over the pad and pen. Without hesitation, Tom scans his eyes down the document, and scribbles his signature. He passes the notepad back, then stares pensively at his lap, breathing heavily.

"Handled," says Lilly. "That's Chrysalis Day funded."

Skun looks on, nodding his head, pensively. "So that's how it's done," he says.

Lilly mimes the word "Tattoo" at Skun, but he doesn't get it, and shakes his head, curiously.

Tom stands, looking at the floor. "I might get some sleep, then." He looks exhausted. His eyes are hollow, and sad. "I, *ummm…*"

"You, what?" Lilly asks.

"I really didn't come back for the money. Lilly."

"*Uh-huh*?"

"I just didn't want to live in a country where you weren't."

Skun Rabbit watches the interaction between Lilly and her husband. She looks at Tom, and she smiles gently. No anger, no anxiety. Just calmness, and kindness, even.

Lilly says, "Good night, Tom."

The Protégé

Three Months Later

Lilly is seated in the front row of the Sydney Opera House. To her left is an empty seat, the left of that is her younger sister Rae. On her right is Skun Rabbit, then Vinnie, then Tom Cata. Tom and Vinnie are chatting away.

Lilly glances around to see that all is well in her world. Everyone is there, that ought to be, save Kara, who has raced off, backstage at short notice. She runs her finger-tip around the back of Skun's hand.

"How's your head?" he asks.

"Sore."

'He chuckles."

"I told you that the needle wasn't intimate."

"You made up for that." She leans over and kisses him on a cheek."

"Get a room," Rae, grumbles.

The curtains on the stage move, and there is a murmur of expectation passes through the packed auditorium. Lilly feels hairs come up on her forearms. The energy in the auditorium is exhilarating. Whatever this thing is, she is in the middle of it; and it's huge.

Vinnie fans herself with the Chrysalis Day event. "I hope this is better than the last show," she says, leaning past Skun Rabbit.

"We'll get a white in the foyer after the event." The lights start to dim, and Lilly glances around. "Where's Kara?" she asks.

"Here she comes, look," Rae says.

Kara hurries down the aisle. She takes her seat next to Lilly, puffing, "Last minute emergency."

"All fixed?"

"Yeah. Hey." She looks up at the stage. "I have always wanted to watch one of my shows. *Ohhh.*"

"What's the matter?"

"What if it's terrible?"

"It will be fine."

Then a young man scurries along the row and parks himself in-front of Lilly. She recognises him, vaguely. Where from? That's right. She saw his face on her intercom. He's the guy who invited her to the flux party on the night.

"Hi, Andy," Rae says surprised. "What are you doing here?"

"Hey Rae," he says, but he's interested in Lilly. He fossicks around inside his dilly bag and retrieves a packet, then holds it out to Lilly. "This is from Froyd."

"Froyd?" Lilly is suddenly alert. She sits up and

turns in her seat to scan the audience. "He's here?"

"Froyd's in the flux, Lilly. He gave me this before he died."

"What is it?"

"It's a package." Andy says, waggling the object.

"Well, I can see that. I mean what is it?"

"How am I supposed to know?" Andy asks abruptly. "He gave it to me and said, give it to Lilly on the opening night of Chrysalis Day. Can't you just take the damned package?"

Lilly complies, and the scrawny young man scurries off. She glances at Kara and Rae and makes an expression that asks, "Do you know anything about this?" Both show blank looks. Lilly inhales deeply and sighs, "*Ahhh,* Froyd."

She tears the flap open and tips the contents onto her lap. There is a folded note and a DVD in an acrylic case. The cover of the DVD reads VITA II. She unfolds the note, seeing that it contains a quarter page of printed text.

The auditorium lights reach their lowest level, and a spotlight plays on the centre of the curtain. Music plays, and the curtains move apart. Onto the stage steps a dynamic young woman. She's dressed impeccably, and well trained in her role.

Kara Lord's protégé opens her arms to the

audience. A shock of curly, black hair wavers as she moves to the centre of the stage, a slim microphone poised in front of her mouth.

"She even looks like you, Kara," Rae says.

"They all do."

"My friends. My dear friends," says the Chrysalis Day presenter. There is a surge of energy, as thirteen hundred people get to their feet in rapturous applause.

"Sustainability & happiness," says Kara's protégé. She shakes her head, knowingly.

"I've trained twenty now," Kara tells Rae, proudly. "And another ten starting next week."

"You'd better get busy," Rae whispers. "The Americans called this afternoon. They're recommending permanent shows in eleven cities."

"Shit," says Kara. "It's really happening." She leans forward, far enough to see Tom Cata, five seats down. "Thanks, Tom," she calls out, with hushed voice, waving.

Tom waves back, bashfully. He's not yet resigned to his new role as the de-facto financier of Chrysalis Day.

Lilly adjusts her glasses and illuminates the note with the glow of her smart phone. The note opens with Lagom, and closes with oOo, which means that it is official Vita correspondence:

Lagom Lilly. If you are reading this, you've had Ecophany, the Lord sisters are back together, and Chrysalis Day is underway. Excellent work.

It's not widely known that the Vita Belief program that you have been guided by – Sustainability and Happiness – is only level one of three levels. Details about Vita II and your instructions are on the enclosed DVD.

All the best, Froyd.

oOo

Lilly slaps the note closed, furious. Damned Froyd Denison! Even when he is dead, he's annoying. She feels the same sense of entrapment and frustration as she did on the day that she smashed the Kintsugi. The feeling quickly changes, and she laughs aloud.

"Everything okay?" Rae asks.

"Everything is as it was," Lilly says.

"*Shhh,*" hisses Kara. "This is the best bit."

On the stage, Kara's protégé settles the crowd with a well-honed movement of her hands, taught to her by an expert. The protégé tells her audience, "You're all living in a bubble. A bubble of gas around our Living Planet."

oOo

www.ingramcontent.com/pod-product-compliance
Lightning Source LLC
Chambersburg PA
CBHW051337020726
47501CB00007B/2125

* 9 7 8 1 7 6 3 5 8 3 4 7 4 *